"A Bland County woman, twenty-three-year-old single mother Teresa Potter, was the winner of last night's five million dollar lottery—"

"Can you believe that?" Judy asked, pointing to the TV hanging from the ceiling. "I mean, she just buys a ticket in the Mini-Mart, and presto, her life is changed overnight."

Willa began filling a row of glasses with iced tea. "Only happens in fairy tales."

Judy reached for a towel and began wiping down the counter. "Does that mean something good can't happen to a person once in a while?"

"No. But I'm not going to stand around waiting for it."

The door opened and Judy's eyes widened. "Don't look now, but the winning lottery ticket just walked in."

Dear Reader,

One of the things that draws me to books is the notion that within the covers of each one exists a group of characters who, like real-life people, have made mistakes, chosen unwisely and maybe found themselves headed in a direction they hadn't anticipated.

In our own lives, mistakes are easy enough, but second chances are sometimes elusive. We don't always get another opportunity to make a better choice. But as readers, we can step into someone else's world, see what happens when they get another shot.

In *The Lost Daughter of Pigeon Hollow*, each of my characters has a problem that needs fixing, a turning point where they must choose to stay as they are or let go of the rope and take a chance. Easier said than done! I hope you'll enjoy watching Owen and Willa give it their best.

I love to hear from readers. Please write to me at P.O. Box 973, Rocky Mount, VA 24151. You can e-mail me at inglathc@aol.com. Or visit my Web site— inglathcooper.com.

All best,

Inglath Cooper

The Lost Daughter of Pigeon Hollow

Inglath Cooper

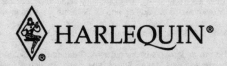

TORONTO • NEW YORK • LONDON
AMSTERDAM • PARIS • SYDNEY • HAMBURG
STOCKHOLM • ATHENS • TOKYO • MILAN • MADRID
PRAGUE • WARSAW • BUDAPEST • AUCKLAND

ISBN 0-373-71263-4

THE LOST DAUGHTER OF PIGEON HOLLOW

This edition published by arrangement with Harlequin Books S.A.

® and TM are trademarks of the publisher. Trademarks indicated with
® are registered in the United States Patent and Trademark Office, the
Canadian Trade Marks Office and in other countries.

www.eHarlequin.com

Printed in U.S.A.

For my grandmothers, Vickie Perdue Holland and
Mary Mullins Johnson, ladies of character and integrity.
I love you more than you can know.

Books by Inglath Cooper

HARLEQUIN SUPERROMANCE
 728—THE LAST GOOD MAN
1174—A WOMAN LIKE ANNIE
1198—JOHN RILEY'S GIRL
1214—UNFINISHED BUSINESS

CHAPTER ONE

PIGEON HOLLOW, KENTUCKY, was the kind of place that could never quite get past its name. No one knew exactly where the name originated. Folks said it had been somebody's idea of a joke. Others said the original settlers in the valley had discovered a flock of albino pigeons that came to symbolize the peace the settlers had hoped to find in their new home.

Nonetheless, the current-day residents of Pigeon Hollow were aware of the initial impression the name conjured. A town full of hicks whose definition of higher education did not broaden past Sugar McWray's Beauty School or the local community college's night course for mechanics.

The town council had proposed changing it a number of times. But the council had never gotten past the talking stage, the consensus being that a town ought to be able to transcend its name.

Mostly, it did.

They had an unemployment factor of less than

three percent; a fair number of their high-school graduates went on to college. In addition, the town boasted impressively high rates of volunteerism and a food bank that stored frozen and canned goods for families in need.

To outsiders, the town was one of those places that existed simply because it was on the road to somewhere else. For Pigeon Hollow, somewhere else was Lexington, and the international horse industry that had become as rooted there as the bluegrass pastures on which equine royalty grazed.

There were those in town who complained about that. Willa Addison wasn't one of them. Except for a few years away at college, she had lived in Pigeon Hollow all her life, and taken over her mama's business when she was twenty-one. A good number of those people driving through to Lexington stopped for a meal at the Top Shelf Diner.

And each of those customers increased the probability that she would be able to pay the monthly stack of bills now looming at one corner of her kitchen counter.

Willa turned her back to the bills, put her hand on the wall-mounted telephone, debating. Should she call or not? Wait a little longer?

Surely, Katie would be home soon.

She'd waited two hours. Long enough that her stomach had begun to feel as if it had a hole in it.

She glanced up at the clock above the sink. Ten minutes past twelve.

And it was a school night.

She dropped her head back, closing her eyes.

She picked up the receiver and punched in Shelby Franklin's number. "Shelby?"

"Yeah?" The response was groggy enough that Willa knew she'd woken her.

"It's Willa. I'm sorry to be calling this late, but Katie isn't home yet. Is Eddie in?"

Shelby let out a sigh, then said, "He don't have to report in to me, Willa."

Exactly. Willa pressed her lips together and counted to three. "Katie was supposed to be home two hours ago. I'm getting a little concerned."

"He ain't living here now, anyway."

Great.

There was the sound of a match striking, a quick puff of a cigarette. "You see, Willa," Shelby said, "that's where you need to open your eyes to reality. If you had any hope of keepin' that child on the straight and narrow, you shoulda' locked her up a couple years back." A crackle of laughter followed the short sermon.

Willa straightened, heat suffusing her face. "You being an expert on successful parenting?"

Shelby chuckled again, as if she enjoyed ruffling Willa's feathers. "I know wild as hell when I see it."

"She's not wild, she's just—"

"Sixteen. Don't be too hard on yourself, sugar," she said, placating now. "You're not her mama. A sister shouldn't have to be walkin' into that role when you did, anyway."

"If you see her, call me back, please." Willa hung up, anchoring the phone to the wall with enough force to rattle her elbow.

The front door opened just then and shut with a bang.

Thank God.

On the heels of Willa's gratitude was an already brewing lecture.

Katie appeared in the kitchen doorway, as casual about her entrance as if it were the middle of the day instead of the middle of the night. A study in rebellion, her hair was cropped short, peroxide blond. A swirl of silver studs covered one ear. She wore a white T-shirt whose bottom just covered her breasts and a pair of boot-cut blue jeans the top of which rode a good two inches below her navel.

She met Willa's stern expression head on. "What?" With extra attitude.

"Where have you been?"

Katie slouched to the refrigerator, opened the door and ducked her head inside. "There's nothing to eat in here."

"You were supposed to be home by ten, Katie."

"So I'm late."

"What were you doing?"

"Studying." The insolence in her voice instantly negated the truth of the answer.

Willa opened the dishwasher, pulled out a clean cup and carefully placed it in the cabinet above. "That's the second night this week, Katie. You're grounded."

Katie dropped a container of yogurt on the kitchen counter and slammed the refrigerator door, rounding on one heel. "God, Willa, will you get over yourself? You're not my mother!"

Hearing that from Shelby Franklin was one thing. Hearing it from Katie was another. Willa suppressed a quick flare of hurt and held out her hand. "Keys to the car."

Katie folded her arms across her chest and glared. "They're in the ignition." She grabbed the yogurt, yanked open a drawer and pulled out a spoon, then stomped upstairs.

The doggy door flapped open from the hallway just off the kitchen. Sam trotted in on his stubby legs, ears lifted in question.

"Heard us from the backyard, huh?"

Sam dropped down on the rug in front of the sink, head on his paws, back legs stretched out behind him. If a dog could wear concern as an expression, Sam wore it clear as day.

His ancestry was questionable. Almost for certain there was Lab in his lineage, accountable for his good nature, Willa suspected. Some beagle as well, judging from his short legs and fondness for rabbit chasing.

He'd shown up at the back door of the diner one winter morning, looking as if he hadn't had a meal in two weeks. It had been Willa's intent to find a home for him, but his affable disposition had mysteriously turned to snarling intimidation whenever she'd shown him to anyone who happened to respond to the posters she'd hung around town.

She'd finally decided to keep him, and he'd been nothing but affable since.

He followed her outside now to her seen-better-days Wagoneer. McDonald's burger wrappers and empty Coke cans littered the floorboard. Cigarette butts stuck out of the open ashtray.

The distinctly sweet odor of something other than tobacco hung in the air. Willa's shoulders slumped beneath a sudden wearing sense of defeat. She pulled the keys from the ignition, picked up the trash, and shut the door.

She tilted her head back, drew in a deep breath. Late May in Kentucky. A neighbor's freshly cut lawn scented the night breeze. A row of sweetshrub divided Willa's driveway from the house next door, adding its fragrance to the mix, the trees lining her street newly green and thriving.

Willa loved spring. Loved its freshness, its promise and the sense she always had of starting over, wiping clean winter's gray slate.

Sam followed her to the front porch where she dropped onto the second step. He lay down at her feet.

Willa rubbed his head, scratching the spot behind his left ear that caused a hind leg to thump automatically.

"Really, Sam," she said, defeat at the edges of her voice. "What am I going to do about her?"

Sam raised his head, whined once. "She's going to end up pregnant or…" She didn't let herself finish the thought.

Sam put his head on her leg and closed his eyes.

"Yeah, I know. That's what I'd like to do. Pretend I don't see it." She massaged the dull ache in her left temple. "But that's not going to work, is it? When I finally do open my eyes, things will just be that much worse."

She glanced up at the dark night sky, chin propped on her hand, elbow on her knee, and stared at the blink of a faraway airplane. She smoothed her other hand across Sam's soft coat, her gaze following the plane's trek below the stars. "Wonder where those people are going."

Sam didn't bother to look up.

"That'd be kind of nice, wouldn't it? Just taking off. Not really even caring where you ended up as long as it was somewhere different. Live another life for a while."

As appealing as it sounded, running away from trouble never worked. During Willa's teenage years, her own mama had tried it a number of times, leaving Katie and Willa alone to fend for themselves. And inevitably, proving that the problems didn't go anywhere. Somebody had to deal with them.

For Willa, the problem was how to steer Katie into adulthood without letting her disappear beneath the too-numerous-to-count sinkholes along the way.

She glanced up at the sky, the airplane now a distant speck. Thought for a moment of her own aspirations, plans she'd put aside to come back to Pigeon Hollow and raise Katie after their mother had died. Those dreams now seemed as far away as the destination of that plane.

She got up from the step, too tired to think about it anymore tonight.

The problems would still be here tomorrow. That, she could count on.

THE TOP SHELF DINER was something of a landmark in Pigeon Hollow. It sat midway down Main

Street, in between Citizens' Bank and Crawley's Hardware.

At eleven in the morning, a sprinkling of customers sat at the square, wooden tables. But within the next forty-five minutes, the place would fill up with the lunch crowd, workers from the sawmill at the other end of town filing in for the daily special: meat loaf and mashed potatoes or corn bread and pinto beans.

Willa stood behind the front counter, filling a pitcher with iced tea. She wiped a hand on her just-above-the-knee black skirt, then glanced up at the TV hanging from the ceiling. It had also snagged the attention of Harold Pinckard and Stanley Arrington where they sat drinking a late morning cup of coffee.

"A Bland County woman, twenty-three-year-old single mother, Teresa Potter, was the winner of last night's five million dollar lottery—"

"Can you believe that?" Judy Parker set a coffeepot back on its burner and scowled at the TV. She pushed her glasses back on her nose, only to have them slide right back to their previous position. Mid-forties, Judy barely broke the five-feet mark, weighed less than a hundred pounds and still managed to be known as a small tornado of energy. "I mean she just buys a ticket in the Mini-Mart, and presto, her life is changed overnight."

Willa began filling a row of glasses with tea. "Only happens in fairy tales."

Judy reached for a towel and began wiping down the Formica counter. "Does that mean something good can't happen to a person once in a while?"

"No. But I'm not going to stand around waiting for it."

Judy made a sound of disapproval, then moved to the sink, rinsed her towel and wrung it out. "So what would you do with it, *if* you believed in the lottery and *if* you won?"

"I don't, and I wouldn't," she said, lifting a shoulder.

"Indulge me. And let's just go ahead and assume you'd give a good portion to your favorite charity. Save the beagles or whatever it is. I want to hear about the you stuff."

Willa smiled. "The me stuff. Okay. I'd buy a black Lamborghini."

"You would not."

"Hey, I thought this was my fantasy."

"Fair enough," Judy said, one hand in the air. "So we have one flamboyant sports car. Proceed."

Willa squinted in thought. "Maybe a nip and tuck at one of those fancy canyon-something spas."

Judy shot her a look, eyebrows raised. "What in the world would you nip and tuck?"

"Decrease size of fanny. Increase size of breasts."

Judy rolled her eyes. "You barely have a fanny. If you go in for that, I'll have to ask for the complete overhaul. So what else?"

Willa pondered for a moment. "My own tab at any Barnes & Noble. Better yet, my own Barnes & Noble with unlimited iced lattes."

Judy made a face. "I never have gotten the whole cold coffee thing."

"Acquired taste," Willa said.

"Apparently. So once you've made the plastic surgeon rich and become the queen of lattes, what else?"

Willa began lining up another row of glasses, quiet for a moment, and then said, "Go back to school, I guess."

Judy reached for the Curel lotion bottle beneath the counter, squirted some on her hands and began rubbing it in. "Dr. Addison. I always did like the sound of that. And you know what? That one shouldn't have to wait around for lottery winnings."

"Yeah, well, the chances of my ever getting to med school are about as likely as my winning the lottery."

"If it's about money, you could always sell this place."

"Right now, I'll be lucky to get Katie through

high school. Med school at the same time? I don't think so."

"You could do it," Judy disagreed.

"Maybe someday," Willa said, hearing the doubt in her own voice.

"Speaking of the teenage terror, did she get home okay last night?"

Willa sighed. "After midnight."

"That girl is gonna make you old before your time."

Willa opened another box of tea bags. "I get a time?"

"Not if you stand around waiting for it." Judy threw Willa's words back at her with a pointed look.

Willa knew better than to get this particular conversation started. "I'll be in the back paying bills."

Thirty minutes later, she closed the checkbook, defeated as always by the dwindling funds in her account. She leaned back in the desk chair and stretched. Sam lay at her feet, snoring.

Katie. Willa hadn't let herself think about her all morning. She'd dropped her off at school without either of them saying a word to each other.

On the subject of her sister, Willa felt as if she'd been dumped out in the middle of the ocean only to discover she couldn't swim. She simply didn't know how to reach Katie anymore.

And if she didn't figure something out fast,

Katie would end up derailing her entire life at the age of sixteen.

The office door opened. Judy poked her head inside, her eyes wide, her smile a little giddy. "To the front, please. Two o'clock."

"What is it?"

Judy made a fluttering gesture over her heart.

Willa gave her a look. "The last time he was a long-haul trucker with the amazing ability to forget he had a wife."

"This is no married truck driver," Judy said. "This is a winning lottery ticket."

Willa shook her head, then smiled and got up from the chair. "Okay. I'll give you the benefit of the doubt."

At the register, she picked up a stack of menus, straightening them. Shania Twain sang on the jukebox.

"Over there," Judy stage-whispered.

Trying to look casual, Willa let her gaze wander to the right-hand corner of the diner. A very good-looking man sat in the booth, rubbing a thumb against a glass of iced tea, a newspaper in front of him. He wore blue jeans and a light blue polo-type shirt. His dark hair was short, and he had nice wide shoulders, well-muscled arms.

"Was I right or what?"

Willa looked back at the man. He was staring

at her. Dead-on. She turned around abruptly and bumped into Judy who was holding a tray of cookies that went flying toward the ceiling. Willa and Judy both juggled for them to little avail. Most landed on the floor. They dropped to their knees behind the register, scooping up cookies and aiming them at a nearby trash can.

Judy gave Willa a smug smile. "Winning ticket, right?"

"I think I'll just crawl back to the office now."

Judy chuckled. "I'm sure he didn't notice."

They catapulted to their feet at the same time. The man stood on the other side of the register, newspaper in hand.

"Ah, sorry," Judy said, looking as if she'd been hit with a stun gun. "All done?"

The man placed the check on the counter. "Yes. It was very good."

Willa swung around and busied herself folding hand towels from the basket on the floor.

"Sure we can't get you anything else?" Judy asked.

"No," the man said. "Would you please tell the owner I enjoyed the meal?"

"You can tell her yourself. Willa?"

Willa turned then, a blush heating her face.

"Willa Addison," Judy said. "She owns the place."

"Thank you," Willa said.

He nodded, holding her gaze for what felt like a moment too long. "You're welcome."

Judy handed him his change. "If you're in town for a bit, come back again."

"I'll do that," he said. He picked up his newspaper and threaded his way back through the diner and out the door.

Judy had the composure to wait until he was outside before dissolving into a puddle. "Oh, my. Oh, my, oh, my. What are you going to do if he comes back?"

"Greet him at the door in a garter belt and fishnet stockings?"

"There's a thought," Judy said with a big grin. "Although, he doesn't seem the fishnet type."

"I wouldn't know what to do with them anyway."

"Not like you've had a lot of practice." Judy hesitated, as if considering what she was about to say. "It's an honorable thing you've done, raising Katie. But does that mean you can't have a life? A man. Your own career choice."

"I *do* have a life. But until Katie is where she needs to be, the last thing I want is another personality in the picture to muddy the waters."

Judy hitched a thumb at the front door. "Even if it comes in that package?"

"Even if."

"And the career thing?"

"I have the diner."

"Not a thing wrong with it if that's what you want."

"I'm not complaining."

"Maybe you should be."

"Judy—"

"Take it from me, honey, the longer you let a dream go, the less likely it is to find you again."

Willa opened the cash register, lifted the drawer and pulled out a stack of checks and receipts, before meeting Judy's gaze head on. "And what about your dreams, Judy?"

"It's a little late for me on that score."

The phone on the counter rang. Willa picked it up. "Top Shelf. Sure, Jerry. She's right here."

Judy took the phone, listened for a few moments. Her expression instantly deflated. "We'll talk about it when I get home, okay?" She punched the off button to the cordless, then handed it back to Willa.

"Everything all right?" she asked, concern threading the words.

"Same ole. Gum stuck to my shoe. No matter how much I'd like to get rid of him, I can't seem to scrape him off."

"You'll scrape him off when you want to."

Willa put a hand on her friend's shoulder and gave it a squeeze. "And by the way, if it's not too late for my dreams, it's not too late for yours."

"Yeah," Judy said, her expression uncharacteristically somber.

"I've got to run to the bank," Willa said. "Back in a few minutes."

"Oh," Judy said, her voice perking up, "if that delectable man comes in again while you're gone, maybe I'll hit on him. How's that for dream fulfillment?"

Willa smiled. "Have at it."

CHAPTER TWO

OWEN MILLER SLID behind the wheel of his dark green Range Rover, shutting the door just as Willa Addison came out of the diner and crossed the street. She never looked his way, so he took advantage of the moment, sat back and watched her.

Medium height. Fair skin. Slim. Straight blond hair, tucked behind her ears, hung to her shoulders.

Very attractive. In those few moments at the register, he had seen Charles in her, mostly the eyes, the high cheekbones.

She stopped to speak to an older woman a half block from the diner. Laughing at something the woman said, she tipped her head back, her hair catching the sunlight.

They talked for a minute or two, and then Willa Addison disappeared through the doors of the bank at the corner.

Owen pulled out of the parking lot and followed the street he'd driven down earlier, spotting the bed-and-breakfast where he'd reserved a room. He turned in, parked out front and grabbed his overnight bag from the back seat.

The owner introduced herself as Mrs. Ross. A round woman, partial to flowers judging by the tulips on her shapeless dress and the magnolia wallpaper lining the foyer and stairwell, she checked him in and directed him upstairs. The room was small, but immaculately clean. The open curtains framed a view of tree-lined Bay Street.

Owen set his laptop up on the desk by the window. He logged onto the Internet, checked his e-mail, took care of a few business-related matters, then opened an e-mail from his brother.

Just thought you'd like to know, the debate continues. See attached.
Cline

Owen downloaded the file. A few seconds later, an article from the *Lexington Daily Record* popped up. His photo accompanied the headline Marriage Or The Farm?

The article below began:

The single days of well-known bachelor and thoroughbred commercial breeding heir Owen Miller may be numbered.

Sources say the will left by his father, Harrison Miller, provides that if he is not engaged by his thirty-third birthday—some ten days from now—Winding Creek Farm and all its subsequent holdings will revert to his younger brother, Cline Miller.

Owen clicked out of the file, disgust hitting him in the gut. He moved the cursor to Instant Messaging and typed in:

You're enjoying this, aren't you?

Cline answered a couple of seconds later:

The entertainment value is huge, you have to admit.

Owen pictured his brother, seated in front of the laptop, and a wave of affection flooded through him.

For you, I suppose.

So, have you found her?

Who?

Your new wife.

I'm not looking for one.

<Big sigh> Just pick out one and get it over with.

Like shopping for a new tie?

The noose-around-your-neck association does not go unappreciated. <grin> You know in the end, Dad always won. And besides, if you hand the mantle over to me, I'm not making any promises about maintaining the family name.

Hmm.

BTW, Pamela called. Again. Have I heard from you? Asked with notable irritation, I might add, leading me to think she hasn't heard from you.

I'll call her.

Good. Unless you find another prospect first. <bigger grin>

Bye, Cline.

See ya.

Owen logged off, leaned back in his chair and laced his hands behind his head. Cline's question wasn't exactly out of left field. Why hadn't he asked Pamela? She expected it, and probably had a right to. They'd been going out for a year. Her expectations weren't unreasonable, considering his position.

When his father died three years ago, Owen had never thought the will provision would actually interfere with his life. It had seemed more of an annoyance, although totally in character, that his father would continue to pull strings, even from the grave.

Maybe Owen had assumed he would be engaged or married by this point, anyway. At least that he would have met someone who made him want to be. But here he was. Time nearly up.

Not married.

He glanced at the phone. He really should call Pamela.

But then there was the red flag. He *should* call her. Later. He'd call her later.

It was the perfect day to be at the lake.

Katie considered pretty much any day perfect if it involved skipping school.

Maybe the principal would eventually give up and just kick her out, putting an end to her useless arguments with Willa. A girl could dream.

A jam box sat at one corner of the dock, D-12 blasting. She could feel the throb of it through the backs of her calves. Beside her, Eddie lay staring at the sky, holding a joint between his thumb and index finger, his expression dreamy. He took another long pull. "God, that's good stuff," he said, his voice raspy with smoke. He passed it to her.

She took a small puff, then handed it back to him.

He laid it on the dock, turned on his side and propped up on his elbow. She looked at him through half-open eyes. He was hot, in a rebel-with-a-cause kind of way. Eddie's cause was whatever pleased him at the moment. A few weeks ago, it had been the hammerhead shark tattoo now etched into his right bicep.

For now, it was her.

He touched her face. "Come here."

She complied, not so much because she wanted to, but because being with Eddie fueled her need to reach for whatever it was she thought would piss Willa off the most.

For now, that was Eddie.

He leaned over and kissed her, heavy duty from the get-go. She followed him for a few moments, and he pushed her back onto the dock, half lying across her. He picked up the pace of the kissing, the lower half of his body moving in suggestion.

Her bikini top slipped. She turned her head,

pulling the bathing suit back in place. "Easy, okay?"

"What? You don't want to?"

Katie raised up on an elbow, dropped her head back and blew out a sigh.

"You've been a real drag all day. Maybe I should have brought someone a little more fun out here."

"Maybe you should have."

Eddie put a hand on her thigh, massaged the muscle, his touch experienced. "Hey, I didn't want to bring anybody else. So what's the deal?"

Katie sighed. "My sister. She's such a pain in the ass."

"She riding you again?"

"Only about everything."

"What's her problem? She's pretty hot-looking for an old girl."

She gave him a look. "Twenty-eight is hardly old."

"You two sure are different."

"That a compliment or insult?"

"Neither. Just seeing her down at the Top Shelf, she acts a lot older than she looks."

"She's been like that ever since Mom died."

Eddie shrugged. "Why don't you just check out of there?"

"And what? Live out of my backpack?"

"Move in with me."

Katie frowned. "And your four other room-mates?"

Eddie brushed the back of his hand against the side of her breast. "Hey, I've got my own bed. That's all we need."

"You are such a jerk."

He lifted an eyebrow. "I'm not stupid. I start acting like Joe Nice Guy, you'll ditch me for sure."

At least he knew her.

Katie stood, shucked off her blue-jean shorts, and made a clean dive into the lake.

Eddie followed. He came up gasping. "Man, it's cold!"

"Weenie."

He kissed her again. "I mean it," he said. "Think about it. Move in with us. We'll have a big time."

She looked at him for a moment, and then said, "I'll think about it."

IT FELT LIKE A REPEAT of the night before. And far too many others in recent weeks.

Willa sat on the living room couch, hands wrapped around a mug of hot tea, a table lamp the only light. Sam was curled up beside her, his head on her leg. A novel lay open on her lap, but she had no idea what she'd read in the last five pages.

She glanced at the grandfather clock on the other side of the room. Eleven.

The front door opened. Katie walked through the foyer and headed up the stairs.

"The principal called," Willa said quietly.

Katie stopped on the second step. "Save it, okay?"

"So what should I do, Katie?" Willa asked in an even voice. "Just let you mess up your life for good?"

"It's not your life to mess up. You're doing a pretty good job with your own."

Willa's grip on the cup tightened. She pressed a finger to her forehead. "How did we get here, Katie?"

"I'm not your responsibility, Willa," Katie said, the words a few degrees softer. "I can take care of myself."

"Is that it, then? Do you think I should let you quit school? Hang out with guys who are going to lead you down the road to nowhere?"

"I'm not as dumb as you think I am."

Willa stood and walked to the bottom of the stairs. "That's not what I think at all. I think you're smart, beautiful and at a very confusing time in your life. But, Katie, the choices you make now are going to affect your future in ways you can't begin to see from here."

"Like the choices you've made, Willa?" She tore up the stairs then, throwing out behind her, "At least I'm out there playing the game."

WILLA DROVE KATIE TO SCHOOL the next morning. Neither spoke the entire way. Katie kept her headset on, the beat of the music pounding like a muted jackhammer.

Willa pulled up at the high school's main entrance. Students loitered around the front steps. "You'll go by the principal's office, Katie?"

"Sure thing."

"Two more absences, and you're going to fail your classes this semester."

"That would be a disaster," Katie said, sounding mildly bored. She got out of the Wagoneer and strolled toward the front entrance, stopping to talk with a trio of defiant-looking teenagers wearing nose rings complemented by varying degrees of purple hair.

Katie had never seemed farther away.

AT THE TOP SHELF, Willa pulled into an empty space beside Judy's old Citation. If possible, it was more of a rattletrap than her own. She got out and waited for Judy who slid out of the car, then slammed the driver's door. The door failed to catch, so she opened it and closed it again.

The sleeve of her white sweater slid up with the movement. An ugly purple bruise encircled her wrist.

Willa touched her arm. "Hey. What's that?"

Judy avoided Willa's gaze. "Nothing."

"Nothing? Judy—"

Judy held up a hand, smiling a little too broadly. "Uh-uh. This problem's not going on your shoulders."

They walked across the parking lot to the diner entrance, both quiet.

"Are you all right, Judy?" Willa finally asked softly.

Judy smiled an of-course smile. "Yes."

"I really am worried about you."

"Don't be."

"How can I not?"

"You know, if they measured worry in a person's blood the way they measure cholesterol and triglycerides, you'd be on the operating table."

"Judy. I'm serious."

"So am I. I'm fine. And we're talking about you, anyway. Now let's hear about those circles under your eyes."

Willa gave in for now. "I don't know what to do with her anymore. It seems like the more I say, the worse things get."

"Maybe it's time to let her fall," Judy reasoned.

"My mama always said she could tell me all day long what a bump on the head was going to feel like, but until my own noggin hit the pavement, there was no way I would ever believe her."

Willa smiled, pushing through the front door of the diner. Clara Hibber, one of the other waitresses, opened up every morning so Willa could take Katie to school.

Clara waved from behind the counter. Willa waved back, then looked at Judy. "She's just so angry. I wish I knew why."

"When you're sixteen, it doesn't matter," Judy said. "Anger is just another hormone. You feel justified. But if anybody should be angry, it's you. You got to be a mother at twenty-one without any of the fun that comes with arriving at that happy state."

"I don't regret what I've done for Katie. She's my sister."

"I know you don't. But for seven years now, you've been living the life of your mother. Taking over this place after she died. You didn't get the chance to be young. Take it from me, the years fly by, and you wake up one day looking at a big sign with Too Late written in big, bold letters."

Willa put a hand on Judy's shoulder. "If that's your subtle way of saying I need a man, I haven't seen anything out there worth missing a night with a good book."

The diner door opened. The man from yesterday walked in, taking the same table as before. Both Willa and Judy stared for a moment. He looked up. They both got busy shuffling menus and stacking coffee cups.

"That's what I call amazing timing," Judy said.

"Just take his order."

Judy grabbed a pad, handed it to Willa, then bolted, whispering over her shoulder, "Ladies' room."

"Judy—"

But she was already out of sight. Willa stared after her, made a mental payback note, then walked over to the table.

The man glanced up.

"What would you like?" she asked, trying not to stare. He was unbelievably good-looking. Dark hair contrasted by light blue eyes. The kind of mouth a woman's gaze could not help being drawn to.

"What do you recommend?" he asked.

"Eggs and bacon are always a sure thing. Pancakes, too, but you don't look like a guy who eats a lot of starch."

"Eggs and bacon, then. But add a pancake, too. I'm feeling like a walk on the wild side."

Willa scribbled the order on her pad, a small smile touching her mouth. "And to drink?"

"Coffee."

She nodded. "Your order will be out in a few minutes."

Judy was back from the ladies' room when Willa got to the front counter. "What did he say?"

"Eggs and bacon. Add a pancake."

Judy snorted. "I really am starting to worry about you. A man like that walks in here, and you don't even flirt with him."

"I said he looked like he doesn't eat a lot of starch. Does that qualify?"

"Struck instant lust in his heart, I'm sure."

Willa smiled, poured coffee in a cup, then carried it to the man's table. He looked up, and she noticed how blue his eyes were. Magnetic, really. She wanted to look longer, but she jerked her gaze away and set the coffee down. "Your food will be right out."

He stood, stuck out his hand. "Owen Miller," he said.

"Willa." She cleared her throat. "Addison."

He stared at her for a moment. "Will you have dinner with me tonight?"

"Dinner? Ah, thank you, but I—" She waved a hand at the diner. "I'm here until pretty late."

"Late is okay."

She stood there, tapping a thumb against the coffeepot. "I take it you're passing through?"

"Can't deny that."

"What would be the point?"

"Conversation?"

For a moment, Willa actually considered it. He was gorgeous, and she was tempted. But her life already had enough complications without pursuing something that would end up going nowhere. She'd already done nowhere. She shook her head. "Thank you for the invitation," she said, "but no."

No.

He hadn't expected rejection. It was the first time in his life he'd ever been turned down by a woman. The thought was completed with no particular amazement; it just wasn't something he was used to. And so, he wasn't exactly sure how to react to it.

Owen took the front porch steps to the bed-and-breakfast two at a time.

Mrs. Ross smiled when he came through the door. "Morning, Mr. Miller."

"Good morning. Do you know what time the Top Shelf closes in the evening, Mrs. Ross?"

The woman gave him a knowing look. "You must have taken a liking to Willa Addison's food. They close at nine."

"Thank you." He hesitated and then said, "What can you tell me about her?"

"What would you like to know?"

"Enough to figure out how to get her to go to dinner with me."

Mrs. Ross chuckled. "Don't know that it'll do any good. Got a load of responsibility with that young sister of hers."

The phone rang. Mrs. Ross reached for it. Owen thanked her and headed up the stairs.

"Young man!" she called out.

He dropped back down a few steps. "Yes?"

"There is one thing I remember about her as a little girl."

"What's that?"

"She loved strawberries."

CHAPTER THREE

HE WAS SITTING ON A BENCH outside the diner when Willa closed up that evening. One leg crossed over a thigh, an arm draped across the back of the bench. Beside him sat a basket of strawberries.

He was the kind of man who made women stop and stare.

Willa stopped and stared.

"I was told you had a fondness for these," he said, picking up the basket and holding it out in one hand.

She started forward with a jolt, tripping on a raised edge in the sidewalk, the library books in her arms cascading to the ground.

He stood instantly, retrieved the books, scanning the covers of each as he handed them to her. "Fitzgerald. Tolstoy. Alternative medicine. Interesting mix."

She eyed him carefully, taking the books from him. "Thanks."

"I asked Mrs. Ross at the B and B how I might

talk you into going to dinner with me. She said strawberries would be worth a try."

Growing up, Willa had picked berries from the patch in Mrs. Ross's backyard every spring. Buckets full, which Willa's mama had put in the freezer for pies and ice cream. "That was nice of you."

"Was she right?"

Willa hesitated. She really shouldn't. She didn't know him. He was passing through. He didn't look like a criminal—quite the opposite, in fact—but then what did that mean? Ted Bundy had been the boy next door with a cast on his leg.

"We can go somewhere public," he added, his voice low and insistent enough to weaken her resistance. "I'll meet you there if that's better. You name the place."

Clearly, he knew his way around women. She shot a glance at the Range Rover parked at the curb. A man like this in Pigeon Hollow? There had to be a catch.

"Are you married?" she asked, failing to keep the suspicion out of her voice.

His eyes widened. "No."

"May I see your left hand?"

He held it out. She looked at the ring finger, then turned his hand over and glanced at the other side. No telltale mark where a ring had been removed.

"Trust issues?" he asked.

"Let's just say you wouldn't be the first man to misplace his wedding band."

He smiled. "Hmm. It's the bad guys that—"

"Give the good guys a bad name." Common sense told her she should go home. But Judy would never let her forget it. And besides, what did she have better to do than wait for Katie to bust her curfew again? Just a few moments ago, she'd felt weary to her heels, dreading the inevitable confrontation. Delaying it suddenly had enormous appeal.

"Now?" she asked, surprising herself.

He brightened. "Now would be great."

"There's a place over off 260."

"I'll follow you," he said, looking just pleased enough to make her heart beat a little faster.

ON THE WAY, WILLA USED her cell phone to call Judy.

Judy's disbelieving shriek pierced her eardrum. "You're meeting him for dinner? I can't believe it."

"He brought me strawberries. I thought I'd better let someone know where I am in case he turns out to be an ax murderer."

Judy laughed. "Yeah, I read the story in yesterday's paper. Well-to-do hunk terrorizing small-town diner owners with poison strawberries."

"It could happen."

"You read too many books. What are you wearing?"

"Black pants and a white blouse. The same thing I wore to work."

"Unbutton a button."

"Judy!"

"It's called sex appeal, honey. You're allowed."

"Thanks," Willa said, laughing, "but I'll keep my buttons buttoned."

"Odds preparation, that's all. Like dropping another five for lottery tickets on the way out of the store."

"The lottery's a scam."

"You're hopeless. You'll call me as soon as you get home?"

"I will." Willa clicked off, then hit the stored button for her home number and got the machine. She left Katie a message, told her she would be home later. They needed to talk.

Maybe by then, Willa would figure out what to say.

THE HOOT 'N' HOLLER DREW a crowd every Friday night for buy-one-get-one-free pitchers of Budweiser and waffle fries.

Willa chose the place because it was one of the liveliest around and not the kind of spot for which she could be accused of harboring any romantic notions.

Even from the parking lot, the noise level required a raised voice. Willa got out and stood beside the Wagoneer. Owen pulled in beside her, the Range Rover making her jalopy of a vehicle look like a third runner-up beauty contestant.

He threw a glance at the front of the building, basically concrete blocks with a roof on it. A big neon sign blinked the name of the establishment in bold orange. "Interesting," he said.

"Not exactly an architectural wonder. But keep in mind the old book-by-its-cover adage."

"Now I'm really curious." He ushered her forward with a wave. "After you."

At the entrance, he held the door for her, and yes, okay, she noticed. Her last few dates—few and far between as they were—had left her all but certain the pool of available men in this county had forgotten any courtesies their mothers had taught them where women were concerned.

The place was nearly full. A country-and-western band took up the far right corner of the room, the lead singer a frosting-kit-era blonde in a miniskirt that redefined mini. She crooned a familiar Reba hit. Smoke hung like a veil over the main room. Peanut shells littered the floor.

The only available table sat a little too close to the band, making conversation next to impossible.

Again, Owen held her chair, waited for her to sit. Again, Willa was impressed. Maybe Judy was right. Maybe she did need to get out more if all it took to wow her was a surface show of manners. Pretty soon, she'd be unbuttoning buttons.

He sat down across from her. "Great place," he said.

"You think?" she shouted.

The band hit the last note of the song and promised to be back in fifteen minutes. A jukebox started up at a volume that did not rattle the eardrums.

"Did you think I'd run when I saw the monster trucks parked outside?"

"I thought the local color might test your resolve."

He smiled. "Did I pass?"

"So far."

"Good."

The waitress arrived with their beer and waffle fries. He poured her a glass from the icy pitcher, then handed her a plate, waited as she put some fries on it. He filled his own glass, loaded his plate and dug in.

She stared.

He looked up, eyebrows raised. "Is something wrong?"

"I—no. You just don't seem like the waffle-fries type."

He took a sip of his beer. "So what do you think my type is?"

She shrugged, buying time.

He sat back and folded his arms across his chest. "No, really. Go ahead."

She wrapped both hands around her glass, giving it some consideration. "Let's see. You play some sport like squash. Or maybe golf. You have a connection to the horse-racing industry. You drink port and smoke skinny cigars."

Owen laughed, a real laugh that came from somewhere deep inside him. "You got one of them right anyway. How'd you figure out the horse connection?"

"We get a lot of that passing through here." She smiled. "And you've got a decal on the back of your truck."

He grinned. "My turn."

Willa wasn't at all sure she wanted to hear the conclusions he'd drawn about her so far.

"So noted you're a reader," he said. "You think TV is the drain through which all modern intelligence is leaking. NPR is secretly programmed on your FM dial. You normally frown on the kind of food sitting in front of us." He hesitated, rubbed his chin, then added, "There's some reason why you're not married. Some obligation you're meeting because a woman like you should have been snatched up long ago. And you've already assigned me a spot in your Okay, so I was right about him file. How did I do?"

She studied him through narrowed eyes. "Did Judy put you up to this?"

He laughed again, one elbow on the table. "Fairly well, I take it."

The band started up with a sudden blast.

Owen leaned over close to her ear. "Since talking is out of the question, how about a dance?"

No was the obvious answer. Again, passing through. Clearly, a one-night thing. And she wasn't a one-night kind of girl.

Intrigued, though? That, she had to admit.

One dance. What could it hurt?

There was a crowd on the parquet floor, making closeness essential. He was a good dancer; she noticed as much right away. Not like he'd had lessons or anything. He just moved with the kind of fluid ease that said the rhythm came naturally.

The frosted-blond singer belted out another Top 40 hit with a lively beat, her gaze set on Owen. Laser set.

Willa didn't think it was her imagination that the woman's hips gyrated with more deliberation every time Owen glanced at the stage.

She couldn't resist. She leaned in and with a straight face, said, "I can duck out. Leave her a clear playing field."

"Do, and I'll stage a food-poisoning picket outside your diner."

"Low."

He smiled. And it hit Willa then that they were flirting with each other. Or maybe she had flirted with him, and he had flirted back. Whatever the sequence of it, she was enjoying herself. Imagine that.

THEY FINISHED THAT SET, and while the band took another break, Willa excused herself to go to the ladies' room.

Owen watched her disappear around the corner. What was he doing? He was supposed to give her the letter. That was all.

He'd asked her to dinner for that purpose alone, and somewhere between the parking lot and that last dance, he'd gotten off track. Way off.

The cell phone in his pocket rang. He pulled it out, hit Send. "Hello."

"Owen."

He looked up at the ceiling. "Pamela."

"Cline said you were going to be out of town for a couple of days," she said, a clear note of dissatisfaction lining her voice.

"Yeah," he said. "Kind of unexpected."

"Is everything all right?" The question tentative, as if she were afraid to ask too much.

"Yes," he said.

"When will you be home?"

"A day or so."

There was a long pause, and then she said, "I'm not really sure how to say this, so I'll just out with it. I haven't made any secret of my hopes for our relationship, Owen. I'm not naive. I realize that if you wanted to marry me, you would already have asked me. So let's just bring this to vote, okay? Propose when you get back, or I'll fade out of the picture. Fair enough?"

"Pamela—"

"You don't need to explain anything. But I can't sit on the fence any longer. That's all." And she hung up.

He sat for a moment, then popped the phone back into his pocket, acknowledging a wash of guilt for the way he had treated her. She didn't deserve it. And she was right. He'd kept her hanging on.

He had come here to do an old friend a favor. Maybe clear his head in the process. And yet he couldn't deny he saw Willa Addison in a light that did nothing to promote either of those agendas.

SHE FELT THE CHANGE as soon as she arrived back at the table. Saw it in the set of his ridiculously well-cut jaw.

Second thoughts.

That was fast.

She glanced down at the top button she'd undone in front of the restroom mirror, her face flushing with instant embarrassment. Initial gut feeling. Always trust it. She'd known this had nowhere to go.

She pasted on a smile, one hand at the neck of her blouse. "It's late. I have to get going."

He stood, threw some bills on the table and said, "Let's go."

She decided to wait until they were outside to clarify that she would be leaving alone.

But as soon as they hit the parking lot, he said, "Is there somewhere we can talk?"

She gave him a smile that had to look as forced as it felt. "Look, Owen. It was fun to this point. But we both know anything more would just be an exercise in why bother. So—"

He leaned in and kissed her, quick and thorough.

At first, Willa was too stunned to respond. But he softened his approach, and anything that might have rallied as outrage collapsed like so much false bravado.

And she responded.

The man knew how to kiss.

She had a moment to catalogue impressions. The very faint scent of expensive cologne. The rough stubble on his chin in direct contrast to his mouth, lips smooth and full. The hand cupping her jaw insistent, but somehow letting her know at the same time, he would stop whenever she wanted.

Never would be just fine.

She finally latched on to enough will to pull back and hope she looked offended. "Why did you do that?"

"Because you're so sure you're right about me."

She raised an eyebrow. "Am I?"

"Not about the obvious, no. Can we sit in your car?"

She dropped her head back, studied the night sky. She finally let her gaze meet his and said, "Why don't we just end this here when we can both still say it was fun?"

"Willa. There's something I need to talk to you about."

The seriousness in his voice brought her up short. "What?"

"Not here. This would be better in private."

"Why can't you say it here?"

A man and woman in twin Stetsons walked by, singing an off-key George Strait tune, slightly drunk smiles on their faces. They both eyed Willa and Owen with curiosity.

"All right," she said and headed for the Wagoneer. She got in the driver's side, the door squeaking in protest. He went around and opened the passenger door, sliding into the seat, making the vehicle seem much smaller. She rolled down her window, feeling a sudden need for air.

"I came here to see you," he said.

The words hung there between them, something in his voice making her stomach drop. "What do you mean?"

He reached in his pocket, pulled out a sealed envelope, handed it to her. "This is for you."

She turned it over. Her name was written in neat cursive on one side. "What is it?"

"A letter. From your father."

She dropped the envelope as if it had suddenly ignited. "What are you talking about?"

"He asked me to come and see you. He's a very old friend of my family."

She slowly shook her head back and forth. "That's ridiculous."

Owen said nothing for a moment. "It's also true."

Impossible. *She* had a father who wanted to see her? Her father had died years ago. And if her mother had been accurate in her portrayal of him, it had been no great loss to the world. "I'm afraid you must have me confused with someone else. My father is dead."

"I don't know what you've been told," he said. "But there's no confusion."

"This has to be a mistake." Her brain tried to process the information, sorted through the bits and pieces her mother had meted out during Willa's childhood about the man who had been her father. Which wasn't much. The one subject Tanya Addison had chosen not to discuss except for the times when Willa's need to know something, anything about her father, pressed her to dole out just enough to stop the questions.

"No mistake," he said.

"If I have a father, why didn't he come himself?" she asked, unable to keep the skepticism out of her voice.

Owen's gaze cut to the parking lot. He rubbed a thumb across the back of his hand, his voice somber when he said, "Because he's sick."

"Sick?"

"He had a very serious heart attack a couple of weeks ago. It was impossible for him to come, so he asked me."

"Why you?"

"I guess I'm someone he trusts."

She gripped both hands on the steering wheel, as if it might steady the tilt of disbelief inside her. "Why now? After all these years?"

"The letter should tell you what you want to know."

Willa picked the envelope up again, stared at the handwriting. "This is why you came here."

"Yes."

"And why you—" She waved a hand at the building they'd just come from, humiliation settling in the pit of her stomach.

"I think that was more about something else," he said, his voice softening. "Something I had no right to pursue."

She wondered what he meant by that, but at the same time did not want to know. He probably had a wife and five kids waiting at home for him. A flat feeling of outrage slid in behind the humiliation.

"Read the letter tonight," he said. "Then we'll talk again."

He got out of the Wagoneer and shut the door with a firm click.

She sat for a few moments, stunned, then finally started the engine and pulled out of the Hoot 'n' Holler parking lot. The Wagoneer muffler clanked on the pavement, a shower of sparks visible in the rearview mirror.

Behind them, he stood, watching her go.

So MUCH FOR well-laid plans.

Owen didn't think he could have bumbled it more if he'd tried.

Willa's reaction to learning about Charles wasn't exactly surprising. She had a father she had not known existed. Who wouldn't be blown out of the water by something like that?

A brown pickup truck with tires that looked like they had been injected with steroids roared into the parking lot, came to a rumbling halt. Two guys in bandanas and muscle shirts got out, swaggered inside.

Owen headed for his own vehicle, got in and slapped a palm against the steering wheel. He had asked Willa out tonight with the intention of softening the news he'd come here to deliver. So how did he explain the detour he'd taken in there with the dancing and flirting? And that kiss in the parking lot. No one had ever accused him of being the straightest arrow around, but he did have a girlfriend, and it wasn't his style to cheat.

Still, there was no getting around the fact that he had wanted to dance with Willa tonight. That he had, without doubt, wanted to kiss her.

He had been around the block enough times to have had a lot of firsts. He'd known his share of women. But the energy between the two of them in there hadn't felt like anything he recognized.

He ran a hand across his face. Or maybe it was just that his back was to the wall, and he was looking for an exit. Ten days to make up his mind. He glanced at his watch. Past midnight. Make that nine days.

The future had never looked less clear.

CHAPTER FOUR

ONE DINNER. One dance. It was always the little decisions that led to the big trouble.

Willa drove a few miles before letting herself glance at the letter on the passenger seat, no idea what to make of any of it.

Owen Miller had been a messenger, a delivery service. His asking her out tonight had nothing whatsoever to do with strawberries, or dancing a shade too close, or anything at all resembling romance.

Cheeks flaming, she fumbled to redo the button of her blouse with one hand.

A date. She'd thought it was a date. And he'd been nothing more than a messenger.

Tipp's Minute Market sat just ahead on the right. Willa hit her blinker, turned in and pulled underneath a parking-lot light. She picked up the letter from the passenger seat, held it for a moment, then began to read.

Dear Willa,

I know you have no idea who I am, and most likely at this point, have no desire to. At least that's what I've been telling myself for too many years to count.

I also know that your mother never told you about me. But I am your father, and I would very much like to meet you.

I sincerely hope you will indulge an old man's wish and return to Lexington with Owen so that we might have a chance to talk.

Sincerely,

Charles Hartmore

It had to be a joke, and yet it didn't read like one.

But it couldn't possibly apply to her. Her father had died. What reason would her mother have had to lie about that?

She flung the letter aside and leaned her head against the seat, a sudden throbbing in her left temple. Crazy. No other word for it.

She put the Wagoneer in gear and pulled back onto the road, parking in the driveway of her house a few minutes later with little memory of how she'd gotten there.

Lights were on. Thank goodness. At least Katie

was here. That was the last thing she needed to deal with tonight.

She stuck her key in the lock and let herself in the front door. Sam bounded into the foyer, tail wagging hard enough to send anything in its path crashing to the floor. She leaned over, rubbed his chin, then went into the kitchen and gave him a bone-shaped cookie from the treat jar. He trotted off, tail flagpole straight.

Music erupted from upstairs, throbbing through the ceiling. The kitchen light fixture rattled in complaint. A drum solo picked up the beat of Willa's headache.

"Katie!"

No answer. No surprise. She climbed the squeaky pine steps to her sister's room, knocking at the closed door. When she got no response, she opened it and stuck her head inside.

Katie had her back turned. She yanked clothes from drawers, tossing them into the suitcases on her bed.

Willa put a hand to her chest, stepped into the room. "Katie."

Her sister whirled then, the surprise on her pretty face quickly replaced by irritation. "Can't you knock?"

"I did." Willa's voice was little more than a whisper.

Katie reached over and lowered the volume on the boom box quaking on her nightstand. "What?"

"I said I did. What are you doing?"

"Packing."

"I can see that."

Katie dropped a handful of thong underwear into the closest suitcase, not meeting Willa's eyes. "Yeah, don't you think it's time we admitted this isn't working?"

"Katie," Willa said, throwing up her hands. "You're sixteen. Where are you going?"

"Eddie said I can stay with him. He's got a place with some friends."

Willa sank down onto the bed, palms on her knees. "Don't do this, Katie."

Katie looked up then, her face blanked of emotion. "I'm not like you, Willa. All you care about is doing the right thing. But we have different definitions of what that is, and I'm not ever going to be like you."

Defiance underscored each word, and Willa's heart wilted beneath the blow. "No one's ever asked you to, Katie. I just want you to give yourself a fair shot."

"Maybe this is the shot I want. Eddie's not so bad."

Willa pressed her lips together, certain that anything negative she said against Eddie would only push Katie out the door that much faster. "Don't you think we should talk about this?"

Katie opened a drawer, scooped up an armful of T-shirts, and hurled them at a suitcase. "There's nothing to talk about. I'm quitting school."

Willa put one hand to the back of her neck. "Oh, Katie, no."

"You quit! Why is it such a crime if I do the same thing?"

"I left my last semester of college. Don't you think that's a little different?"

"Is it? Sometimes I wonder if you really wanted to stay here or if it was just a good place to lock yourself up."

Willa pressed two fingers to the bridge of her nose where a sudden pain had set up. "My coming back had nothing to do with that," she said in a calm voice.

Katie reached for another shirt, tossed it in the suitcase. "You're sure about that?"

Frustration at her sister, for her sister, churned inside her. "This isn't about me, Katie! It's about you. I know this may seem like what you want right now. But believe me, one day you're going to wake up and wish you'd taken a different path."

"You'd know about that, wouldn't you?"

Willa flinched, the question hitting its intended mark. "I don't regret what I've done."

"But then we're not all saints." Katie propped her fists on her hips, her blue eyes narrowed. "I mean what about all those dreams you had? Don't you ever wonder what kind of doctor you would have made?"

Willa wrapped her arms around her waist, anger a sudden weight on her chest. It wasn't often that she let Katie get to her, but tonight her defenses were down. "What do you think I should have done, Katie? Left you to foster care? Pretended you weren't my sister?"

Katie glared at her. "Yeah, maybe so. Then at least one of us would have had a chance to be happy."

Hurt flared inside her, spread like liquid fire. There didn't seem to be anything she could say to soften Katie's resentment. And wasn't that the ultimate irony? That Katie was the one harboring all the regret?

Suddenly, Willa couldn't talk about this anymore. "You're not going anywhere tonight, are you?"

Katie stubbed a sneakered toe against the worn rug beside her bed and shoved her hands in the pockets of her faded jeans. "No."

Under a stifling sense of failure, Willa turned and left the room, closing the door with a satisfying thud.

Downstairs, Sam finished up the remains of his bone. At the sight of her, he stood, whined and wagged his tail. The dog was nearly human, and it wasn't the first time Willa had glimpsed sympathy on his face. She grabbed her purse from the table in the foyer. "Come on, Sam. I could use a change of scenery."

He was out the door in a flash, as if he, too, needed the escape.

OWEN HAD JUST LET HIMSELF into his room when his cell phone rang. His home number flashed on caller ID. He clicked on to an unusually somber Cline.

"Natalie just called," he said. "Charles is in the hospital again."

"What?"

"Yeah, it looks like he might have had another heart attack."

Owen's grip on the phone tightened. "How serious is it?"

"I'm not sure. Natalie was pretty out of it. I don't know more than that. She asked where you were. I didn't know what to tell her, so I just said out of town."

He pushed a hand through his hair. "Okay. I'll head home."

"Tonight?"

"Yeah."

"Drive safe."

Owen hung up, stunned. Willa. Charles hadn't met Willa yet. The very real possibility that he might die without doing so flooded him with a sinking sense of panic. He yanked his suitcase out of the closet, started throwing things inside.

He had to get back. And somehow, convince Willa to go with him.

WILLA DROVE, her mind going in a dozen directions.

Sam sat on the seat next to her, alternating between looking ahead and then out the window.

She followed the street through town, edging out into the county until she ended up at Judy's. She pulled into the driveway and cut the lights. The house was small but neatly manicured, bushes trimmed. Baskets of ferns hung from the porch roof above a newly painted white railing.

Crossing her fingers that Jerry wouldn't answer the door, Willa knocked. She waited a few moments, decided this had been a crazy idea and tripped back down the steps.

The door squeaked open. Willa turned around, and there stood Judy with a batch of pink and blue curlers in her hair, her eyes and mouth the only visible landmarks beneath a glacier of cold cream.

"I'm sorry. I shouldn't have come."

Judy waved a hand in front of her face. "Yeah, I know. It's not pretty."

Willa tried for a smile. "Have you got a minute?"

"Do you really think I'm going to let you leave without telling me what brought you out here at this hour?" She pulled the door closed and sat down on the top porch step.

Front paws on the dashboard, Sam barked his displeasure at being left in the car.

"So shoot," Judy said.

Willa sat down, then sighed. "I don't even know where to start."

"How about with the date? How was it?"

She massaged the back of her neck with one hand, the tension there a hard knot. "First of all, it wasn't a date."

Judy raised a skeptical eyebrow. "By whose definition?"

"All concerned parties. Believe me."

"Oook-kay. How about starting at the beginning?"

Willa stared at the step beneath her feet. "He came here to tell me I have a father in Lexington."

Judy's eyes popped wide. "Whoa."

"Yeah. I know."

"Are you serious?"

"He sent a letter saying he knows my mother never told me about him."

Judy shook her head, pink sponge curlers jiggling. "Why?"

"I have no idea."

"So what now?"

"Nothing, I guess."

"Don't you want to meet him?"

Willa lifted a shoulder. "No. I mean, I don't know. The whole thing is just too weird."

"What if he's rich?"

"Judy."

"Maybe you're his only heir, and he wants to leave you the millions he no longer has any use for."

"The lottery thing again."

Judy smiled. "All joking aside, of course you have to meet him."

"Why? What difference would it make now?"

"Because if you don't, you'll wonder about it for the rest of your life. That's a long time to wonder."

"I've managed twenty-eight years without him."

"But that was before you knew he existed. That changes everything."

Willa considered the words, wondering if Judy might be right.

"And our delectable Kentucky morsel. Where does he fit into all this?"

"Apparently, he's an old friend of my—" She broke off there, unable to say the word. "I guess the whole dinner thing was just a big setup."

Judy rewound a wayward sponge curler. "So you didn't have any fun?"

"That's not the point."

"What's that old saying? Don't shoot the messenger?"

"The messenger could have just given me the letter sans the dinner and dancing."

"Me? I would have preferred his version. You know, Willa, you're way too young to be writing off the entire male population. Like me, you just picked wrong the first time around. Unlike me, you can still do something about it."

Willa put one elbow on her knee, palm to her forehead. "I've got bigger stuff to worry about."

"Let me guess. Katie."

She nodded, miserable. "When I got home tonight, she was packing. She's planning to quit school and move in with Eddie."

Judy rolled her eyes. "Hormones must actually leech intelligence from the teenage brain."

"She's just so unhappy," Willa said, shaking her head. "I don't know what to do."

"Maybe you're going to have to let her make

the mistake. It's kind of like quicksand. Once you get out in the middle of it, it's not that easy to remove yourself."

Willa stared up at the sky. "I don't know."

They sat there for a few minutes, not talking. Finally, Judy said, "Okay, here's the fix. Go to Lexington, meet this man, and take Katie with you. Get her away from here a while. Maybe that's all it will take to make her see young Eddie in a different light."

"She seems pretty hooked on him."

"That old saying, absence makes the heart grow fonder?" She flapped a hand. "Hogwash. Out of sight, out of mind."

OWEN HAD BEEN WAITING in Willa Addison's driveway for a little over an hour when the Wagoneer rattled to a stop behind him. He got out of the Range Rover and waited for her.

She opened the door. A small beagle mix leaped out ahead of her, rocketing toward him like a mini torpedo.

"Sam, no!" Willa called out, jumping from the Wagoneer.

The dog latched his teeth on to Owen's pants, his four legs planted like concrete columns. He growled and shook his head, looking over his shoulder at Willa for confirmation of his catch.

She bent to rub the dog's back. "Let go, Sam."

He did so with reluctance.

"I'm sorry," Willa said, looking up at Owen. "He's a little protective."

Owen reached down and rubbed his ankle. "Is that so?"

"He's really a teddy bear. Except when it comes to looking out for me. The only flaw is he doesn't know a good guy from a bad guy."

Owen let that hang a moment, then said, "At least he spared me my skin."

She glanced at her watch, gave him a questioning look. "It's two in the morning."

"Ah, yeah." He ran a hand through his hair. "Something's come up. It's Charles. He's in the hospital again."

Willa stared at him for a moment. "What happened?"

"The doctors are guessing another heart attack. I don't know very much. But I'm heading back tonight to see him. I was hoping you would come with me."

"Tonight?" She put a hand to her chest. "I'm sorry. I couldn't possibly—"

"Look, Willa. I know this is all kind of crazy. I don't want to sound like I'm pressuring you, but anything could happen. He's a good man who's looking to fix something he regrets. Can't you just give him this chance?"

Her eyes softened. White teeth worried her bottom lip. "Even if I wanted to, I can't go tonight." She hooked a thumb at the house. "My sister. She's having a tough time. I need to be here for her."

"Sixteenish? Blond?"

"Yeah. Why?"

"She left a little while ago with a couple of suitcases."

"What?" Willa whirled and ran to the house, taking the porch steps two at a time. The dog was right on her heels, barking like he'd just gotten a good rabbit scent.

Owen followed, opening the screen door and letting himself inside. He could hear her hurried footsteps upstairs, the beagle's click-click-click behind her.

He waited in the foyer. A minute later, she came back down the stairs, her steps heavy, her expression defeated. He followed her back outside where she sat down on the bottom step of the porch and released a heavy sigh.

"Did you see who she left with?" she asked.

"A couple of guys in an old white Buick."

"Eddie."

"Boyfriend?"

"Boyfriend."

"I take it you didn't know about this?"

"She was threatening to leave, but she said she wouldn't go tonight."

"Teenagers."

"Look, Owen. I can't go with you. Not now. I'm sorry about…your friend. But I have responsibilities here."

Wondering if he were crazy to make the offer, Owen forged on before he had time to consider whether it made any sense. "Do you know where she is?"

"I'm pretty sure I do."

"Okay. So here's the deal. Go pack your stuff, and we'll pick up your sister. She can go with us."

Her eyes widened at the suggestion. "I don't think she will."

"This guy she left with. I take it you'd rather she hadn't left with him?"

"She doesn't really care what I think."

"Then call it an intervention."

"That *is* crazy."

The cell phone in his pocket rang. He flipped it open to Cline's somber voice. "Hey," Owen said. "How is he?"

"I went to the hospital. Natalie is over the top."

"I'm heading back, Cline. If she calls again, tell her I'll be there as soon as I can, okay?"

"Okay," he said.

Owen hung up and looked at Willa. "That was my brother. Charles's wife, Natalie, she's having a tough time. I really have to get back. Are you coming or not?"

Indecision wavered across her face. The soft drone of an airplane engine broke the silence. She glanced up at the sky, then stood suddenly. "Give me a couple minutes. I'll be right down."

CHAPTER FIVE

THIS WAS NUTS.

No other way to look at it.

Willa jammed clothes into the tired blue Samsonite suitcase she'd inherited from her mother, not giving herself time to think about what she was doing. To do so would be to call a halt to the whole thing.

Maybe it was crazy, but this man who claimed to be her father could die at any minute. And if he did, Judy might be right. Maybe she would spend the rest of her life wishing she'd had the chance to meet him. To look in his eyes and see if there was truth there.

She picked up the phone on her nightstand and dialed Judy's number. This time she wasn't so lucky. Jerry answered with a growl.

She started to apologize for calling in the middle of the night, decided she didn't want to be that nice to him and said, "May I speak to Judy?"

There was a rustling sound and then a clunk, as if the phone had been dropped.

"Hello?"

"You were asleep," Willa said.

"Um, yeah. It would seem you're not into that tonight."

"Sorry. It's just that I've decided to go."

"To Lexington?"

"Yeah."

"Well, glory be." More awake now.

"It's probably going to be a mistake. But Owen got a call that Charles—this man who says he's my father—he's in the hospital. It may be serious. And Katie's run off with Eddie. I don't know, it just seems like maybe there's some kind of timing in all this."

"If you're calling to see whether I'll take care of the diner, don't bother asking. Of course, I will."

Willa sighed in relief. "Judy, you're the best."

"I'd like regular updates, of course."

"Absolutely. Okay. I'll talk to you soon." Willa hung up. She had to find some way to pay Judy back.

She latched the suitcase and lugged it down the stairs. Owen met her at the bottom.

"I could have gotten that for you," he said.

"It's not that heavy. I'll be right back."

She ran into the kitchen, grabbed a few cans of Sam's food from the pantry and met Owen outside by the Range Rover where he'd already tucked her suitcase in back.

"I went ahead and moved your vehicle. Hope that was all right."

"Thanks."

He eyed the cans and said, "Let me guess. You can't leave without—"

"Sam," she said, looking down at the dog now postured in a perfectly obedient sit at her side.

Owen waved a hand at the door. "Hop in, Sam."

Sam didn't wait for a second invitation. He jumped in the back seat. As soon as he made sure Willa got in the front, he curled up and closed his eyes.

Owen started the vehicle. "Next stop, Katie?"

Willa nodded, her stomach in knots.

"Directions are all I need."

IT LOOKED LIKE THE KIND of place where people got shot. Rundown once-white clapboard house. Shutters hanging askew. Front yard doubling as a cemetery for junk cars and their assorted body parts: a stack of old tires, some rusted bumpers.

Willa had agreed to wait in the car while Owen went to the door. He was starting to think this hadn't been such a great idea. He'd left his white horse at home in the barn, and he didn't have a thing on him that could be considered protection except his fists.

Willa was right to be worried sick about her little sister. This wasn't exactly the kind of place where a sixteen-year-old girl ought to be socializing.

No lights on save the single bulb dangling above the front door. Owen tripped over something, then turned to look back. An old car battery.

He rapped lightly at the door. From out back, a tomcat yowled.

Stumbling sounds arose within the house, followed by a muffled, "Yeah, what do you want?"

"I'd like to speak to Katie."

"She's not here."

"Are you Eddie?"

"So what if I am?" Irritation drew the question tight.

Owen pressed a hand against the doorjamb, studied the less-than-sturdy porch flooring. "I have reason to believe she's here, Eddie."

The door blasted open. A grizzled teenager glared out at him. He wore nothing but a pair of plaid boxers and a set of brass knuckles.

Owen's gaze lingered on the latter. "Hey, look, I'm not here for trouble. We'd just like to speak to Katie for a minute."

"So you can talk her into leaving? She's here because she wants to be here."

Owen held up a hand. "I know. Her sister just wants to know she's all right."

"Who is it, Eddie?"

Behind him appeared the young blonde Owen had seen earlier, now dressed in boxer shorts and an Abercrombie & Fitch T-shirt, her feet bare.

"Somebody's here to see you," Eddie said, not bothering to hide his sarcasm.

"Are you Katie?" Owen asked.

The girl stepped forward. "Yeah. You're the guy in the driveway. Who are you, anyway?"

"I'm with your sister."

Surprise diluted the sullenness on her face. "She's here?"

"Yeah. Could you just come out and talk to her for a minute?"

"We don't have anything to talk about."

Didn't look like this was going to be easy. "Katie," he said, appeal in his voice. "She just wants to make sure you're all right."

The girl looked down at the mud-brown carpet beneath her feet, a curtain of blond hair covering her face.

"Time for you to go, okay?" Eddie warned in a low growl.

"Katie? Just for a minute. Then you can do whatever you want—"

Eddie shoved Owen backward. "You don't listen too good, man."

Owen hadn't been in a fight since his teenage

years, but he itched to punch this cocky jerk in the mouth. He restrained himself. Barely.

"Eddie!" Katie said. "Just stay here, okay? I'll be right back."

Owen stepped off the porch, Katie following him. He looked back. Eddie had disappeared, but the door was still open.

All the way across the yard, Owen told himself this was asking for trouble. The night hung dark and damp, a few stars in the sky. A dog barked at the house across the road. He'd really been hoping Katie would dump Eddie and decide to go with them on her own. He was beginning to realize exactly how unlikely that was.

At the Range Rover, he opened the back door. "Get in for a minute. It's kind of cool out here."

Katie looked inside at Willa, then back at Owen. "You're not just here to talk, are you?"

"Katie—" Willa's voice held a note of appeal.

The girl jumped back, turned to run. Owen hooked an arm around her waist, picked her up and plopped her in the back seat. "Hit the lock, Willa!" he said, slamming the door.

There was a fumbling sound, and then the locks engaged with a thunk.

Katie yanked at the door handle. "Let me out!"

Owen's door was open, and he slid inside. He started the engine and made a spinout U-turn.

"Stop!" Katie screamed. "You can't do this, Willa! You have no right!"

Owen glanced in the rearview mirror. Eddie in full sprint across the yard, a rifle in his hand.

Owen hit the gas.

A loud pop sounded from the exterior of the Range Rover.

Willa screamed. Sam started barking to raise the dead. Owen drove like the devil himself was after them, praying no one had been hit.

THEY STOPPED A HALF MILE or so up the road.

"He shot at us," Willa said, still too numb to believe what had just happened. The whole thing had been a mistake to start with. She should have known better.

Owen got out, walked around to the rear of the vehicle. He got back in, looked at Willa and said, "The bullet hit the bumper. Are you all right?"

"Yes." Willa unhooked her seat belt, her hand still shaking. She turned to look at her sister. "This is crazy, Katie."

Katie sat with her arms folded across her chest, face to the window, her jaw set. "Oh, and you kidnapping me isn't?"

"He could have killed one of us!" Willa's voice shook with anger and disbelief.

Sam whined, scooted across the back seat on his belly, put his head on Katie's lap.

Willa looked at Owen. "I'm so sorry. I never thought any of that would happen."

"Hey, it's over. Let's just get on down the road, okay?"

"Maybe you should take us back home."

"See Charles, and then I'll bring you back. That's fair, don't you think?"

Willa looked down at her lap. "I don't know. It all seems a little out of hand."

"Hopefully, that's the last of the gunslinging."

Katie banged on the back window. "Let me out! I'm not going anywhere with you."

"Sit tight," Owen said in a voice that allowed no room for argument.

Its effect on Katie was amazing. She sat back in the seat, arms folded across her chest, glaring, but without saying another word.

"Okay. Let's go," Willa said, praying that in this case, the end really would justify the means.

THEY DROVE for two hours.

Katie sat rigid as a statue in the back seat, refusing to speak, no matter how many times Willa tried to engage her in conversation. She had to wonder where they were going and what all of this was about, but she refused to ask. And Willa decided maybe it would be better to wait and tell her once she knew a little more herself.

Owen drove without talking, as well. He'd turned on the radio to one of those stations that played jazz without commercials. Willa leaned her head back and closed her eyes, suddenly too tired to think about what she had just done and what might be ahead.

She awoke some time later to a hand on her arm. "Hey, we're here."

She sat up. "Oh. I fell asleep."

"Katie's out, too. I thought we could drop her off before going to the hospital since she doesn't have any clothes."

Willa stretched, then turned to check Katie who was asleep, her hand resting on Sam's back.

She looked out the window. The sun was just starting to rise, pink streaks highlighting the sky. "Where are we?" she asked.

"At my house."

"Oh," Willa said, glancing at the pastures flanking either side of the driveway.

A two-story stone house sat directly in front of them. White shutters framed the windows. Twin oaks, at least a century old, graced each corner of the house. Enormous boxwoods rimmed the perimeter. A walkway curved from the driveway through the yard to the front door.

White board fencing angled out in every direction, horses grazing on green grass. Several hundred yards away stood a huge gable-roof barn. A man on a John Deere tractor scooped sawdust from a shed.

"That's Jake," Owen said, tipping his head at the man. "He can watch after Katie while we're gone."

Willa ran a hand through her hair, certain she must look like a train wreck. "I can't just lock her up."

"Right now, I'm not sure you have a choice unless you want her to head right back to our young friend Eddie."

The image of that bullet zinging toward them was enough to make her nod and say, "Okay."

"We can go inside for a minute, if you'd like to freshen up."

"Actually, that would be nice." Willa went around and opened Katie's door, putting a hand on her sister's shoulder. "Hey, Katie. Wake up."

For a moment, Willa saw a younger Katie in her sister's relaxed features, and yearned for a time not so long ago when she had looked to Willa for everything. Katie made a noise of protest, turned her head to the side as if she could burrow deeper into sleep, then bolted upright. "Where are we?"

"We're at Owen's house. You're going to stay

here for a little while. I have to go see someone, and then I'll be back."

"You can't just leave me here, Willa!" Wide awake now and indignant. "I could call the police!"

"Katie, this is for your own good," Willa said. "Try to believe that. Please?"

Owen stepped up beside Willa. "You can follow me," he said.

Katie slid out of the vehicle, looking wounded and belligerent. She marched after Owen. Willa signaled for Sam to get out, and he leaped across the grass, tail wagging full force.

She stood for a moment, staring after the trio, feeling as if she'd stepped out of her own life and into someone else's.

WILLA HAD COMPLETELY lost it.

Katie could find no other explanation for it. She'd dragged her off against her will and then dumped her in this room with the warning that there was a man downstairs to stop her if she tried to leave.

As jail cells went, the place wasn't that bad. What little she'd seen of the house on the way in was like something out of a fancy architectural magazine. The foyer alone the size of most people's living rooms. The staircase one of those winding jobs with about a million steps.

The room in which she'd been left was a teen-ager's fantasy. A dark wood four-poster bed, queen size, sat in the center of the room. The com-forter looked like the big down-filled kind she'd seen in the Chambers catalog they'd gotten in the mail a couple of times, and her bones ached for sleep just looking at it.

A modern-looking TV sat inside an oversize entertainment center, a flat-screen computer on a desk just to the right of it.

Katie went to the window, folded her arms across her chest and looked out at the sight below. The barn looked like a busy place. Sleek horses being led out to pastures. A John Deere Gator loaded with bags of grain disappearing inside the big sliding doors at the front.

What was Willa doing here? How did she know someone who owned a place like this? And where had she gone?

Patience wasn't one of Katie's strong suits. She wanted some answers, and she wanted them now. But short of hurling herself out the window, she had little choice but to stay put.

She glanced at the clothes on the bed. Boring. Willa had left her with some of her own since Katie had nothing but the T-shirt and boxers she'd been wearing when she'd been abducted.

No way could there actually be a guard at the

front door to keep her from leaving. She reached for Willa's jeans.

She'd just have to go see for herself.

THEY DROVE FOR THE FIRST few minutes in silence.

Owen had set Sam up in the kitchen with Louisa, a round-faced woman who introduced herself to Willa as the "one who feeds everyone around here," and then to Sam with a slice of turkey still warm from the oven. Instant adoration on Sam's part.

Willa's brain felt fuzzy now with lack of sleep, and the situation continued to grow stranger to her by the minute.

Owen pushed the upper edge of the speed limit, driving with his hands clasped tightly on the wheel, a deeply worried look on his face. "Is everything all right?" she asked.

He stared straight ahead, his voice somber when he said, "While you were changing, I called Natalie at the hospital. Charles isn't doing well."

Something tight formed a sudden clamp around Willa's chest. She'd never met Charles Hartmore, would not know him if they passed each other on the street, but already he had made an impact on her life. If only by the very possibility that he might be her father. She turned her gaze to the window and tried to focus on the beautiful horse farms rolling by.

They drove a few miles in silence before she spoke. "Can you tell me something about him?"

"Yeah, sure," he said, glancing at her. "He's been sort of an uncle to me. He and my dad shared some business interests. Charles inherited his family's horse-breeding business. Maple Run Farm is well-known in the racing world. I guess I've known him most of my life."

"When did he tell you about me?"

Owen glanced at her. "Just a couple days ago."

"Does he have other children?"

"No."

She said nothing for a moment, and then, "And apparently never wanted any."

"Willa—"

"I don't know what could possibly be said to rationalize any of this."

"Maybe that's not the point," he said softly.

"What is the point then?"

"Resolution?"

"Twenty-four hours ago, the only thing I knew about my father was that I was probably better off that he never hung around. My mom painted a pretty clear picture of him. Not a favorable one."

He shot her a glance, one elbow on his windowsill, the other on the steering wheel. "I'm not making excuses for Charles, but maybe there's something to be gained in hearing his side of the story."

She folded her arms across her chest and stared out the window. "When I was a little girl," she said in a barely audible voice, "I used to imagine what it would be like to have a daddy. We'd be at the park, and I'd see these fathers playing piggyback with their daughters. Those girls, they just had this look, this deep happiness on their faces, like something I'd never felt before."

A tractor trailer passed them on the other side of the road, throwing up a whoosh of rain from an early morning shower.

Owen put a hand over hers, squeezing hard. "I wish this could have happened sooner for you both."

"Yeah," she said. "But it didn't."

CHAPTER SIX

AT BARELY 7:00 A.M., the hospital was hushed and quiet, doctors and nurses arriving and departing in a shift change. Willa and Owen took the elevator to the fourth floor, stepped out in front of the check-in station. The antiseptic smell tilted Willa's stomach, made her blink against a sudden wave of dizziness.

She steadied herself with a hand to the wall.

Owen turned and put an arm around her shoulders. "Are you all right?" he asked.

"Yes, I…yes."

He told the nurse at the front desk which room they were looking for, and she pointed them to the right.

Owen kept his arm in place all the way down the hall, and Willa could not deny being grateful for his quiet strength.

They stopped in front of room 405. He knocked softly. A tall woman with a thin, angular face stepped out, her eyes red-rimmed and weary. Despite her obvious fatigue, she still managed to look completely put together, flawless French manicure, her white sweater and navy pants free of wrinkle or crease.

Owen pulled her against him, folded her up in his arms, kissed the side of her head. She sobbed softly, as if she had been holding it in for a long time. Willa glanced away.

They stood that way for a couple of minutes, Owen rubbing the woman's shoulder, offering soft words of comfort.

She stepped back, reached in the pocket of her trousers and pulled out a tissue, wiping her eyes.

"Natalie, this is Willa Addison."

"Hello," Willa said, sticking out her hand.

The woman put her hands in her pockets, her gaze cooling several degrees. "I know who you are."

Willa dropped her hand, feeling the sudden scorch of rejection. "I'm sorry," she began and then stopped, not sure what she was apologizing for.

Natalie Hartmore looked at Owen. "Did Charles send you to find her?"

Owen put a hand to her elbow. "Natalie—"

"Just tell me," she said, her mouth drawn tight.

"Yes," Owen said. "He did."

Willa took a step back. "I should go."

The older woman drew in a deep breath, placed two fingers to her lips as if trying to hold back another onslaught of tears. "I'm going downstairs for a cup of coffee. I'll be back in a few minutes."

She turned then and walked down the hall. Once she'd reached the corner in the corridor, Owen looked at Willa and said, "Please don't take any of that personally."

Willa shook her head. "I shouldn't be here."

"Yes," he interrupted, a hand on her arm. "You absolutely should be. Go inside and see him. I'll wait out here."

She felt light-headed with a sudden sense of panic. This was wrong. Natalie Hartmore's reaction was proof of that. "I don't think I can," she said, one hand to her chest.

Owen reached out, tipped her chin toward him. "He would very much want you to. Shouldn't that be what matters now?"

They looked at each other, his eyes dark with compassion. In that moment, she glimpsed something in Owen Miller she had not yet seen.

"Regret is one thing we can't fix," he said. "I know Charles regrets not having you in his life. If you can't do this for him, then do it for you. So you don't have anything to regret."

True enough that this opportunity might never present itself again. A half-dozen emotions swirled like a kaleidoscope inside her. Prominent among them, a sudden need to put a face to the word *father,* fill in the blank space in her thoughts when she wondered about him.

She owed him nothing, but she would do this for herself. She pushed open the door and stepped inside the room.

OWEN STOOD BY A WINDOW, looking out across the small park to one side of the hospital, thinking about that subject of regrets. He had a backlog of his own where his father was concerned. And yet what could he have done to change any of it, make it turn out differently?

What he had wanted from his father, Harrison Miller had never been able to give. It hadn't been in him to do so.

"Hey."

Owen turned from the window. Pamela Lawrence stood at the edge of the carpeted floor, looking uncharacteristically uncertain of her welcome. Confidence was as much a part of her genetics as the Austrian ancestry responsible for her high cheekbones and blue eyes. "I was on the way to a league meeting," she said, running a hand across the black-and-white skirt of her designer suit. "I called Natalie earlier. She told me you were coming by."

"Yeah." Owen said, his shoulders suddenly tense.

She stepped forward then, leaned in and kissed him. She touched the tip of a manicured finger to his mouth, then turned away, tucking her straight blond hair behind her ear. "I'm really sorry about all this. I know how fond you are of Charles."

"Thanks." Owen felt the strain between them, knew he was responsible for it, and yet he couldn't bring himself to address it. He glanced at the door of Charles's room, thought of Willa alone in there and wished, suddenly, that he had gone in with her.

"I wanted to apologize about that phone call," Pamela said. She looked down and then met his gaze. "I'm not trying to pressure you, Owen."

"I haven't been exactly fair to you," he said.

She shrugged, her expression not one of disagreement. "I care about you."

Natalie returned just then with a cup of coffee, which she handed to Owen.

"Thank you," he said.

Natalie looked at Pamela. "I would have brought you some had I realized you were here."

"I already had a cup," Pamela said, waving away the offer. "I'm so sorry about Charles."

Natalie nodded, sat down in a chair close to the window and stared straight ahead, her hands clasped around the paper cup.

Pamela looked at Owen. "Call me later?"

"Yeah," Owen said.

She touched his arm, then left. He drank his coffee, relieved.

WILLA STOOD BY THE HOSPITAL BED, her gaze locked on the man lying too still against the white sheets.

Her heart knocked hard in her chest, and her hands felt clammy. She laced them together, sat down in the chair beside the bed, suddenly unsure her legs would support her.

Machines surrounded him, the intermittent beeps startling in the quiet. His eyes were closed, and at first Willa was afraid to look at him. Afraid of what she might see. Or that he would awaken and find her staring.

But he was still, his breathing a shallow rise and fall. She looked at him then, saw a tired man with white hair and heavy, dark eyebrows. He had a strong jaw, a straight nose, and he looked as if he might have been imposing in the prime of his life.

He opened his eyes, silent for several moments, as if he were trying to bring her into focus. She saw the recognition the second it hit his face.

"You're Willa, aren't you?" His voice was low and strained.

She glanced down, then met his searching gaze. "I, yes."

"Ah," he said, reaching for her hand. "You look so much like her. Beautiful."

If she had entered this room with doubts about the truth behind his request to see her, they instantly dissolved beneath the sincerity in his voice.

"Thank you," she said.

"You're very kind to come here…like this." His voice was weak, as if each word required an inordinate amount of strength.

"Maybe you should rest," she said, starting to stand. "I can come back in a little while."

"Dear child, no," he said, putting a hand on her arm. "There's nothing left that I must do, other than this. Please, stay."

Willa sat back down, pressed her lips together against an unexpected rush of emotion. "Is there anything I can get you?"

"A small sip of water would be nice."

She reached for the yellow pitcher on the bedside tray, poured a cup and handed it to him. His hand shook, and he nearly dropped it.

"Let me help," she said, steadying the cup and then holding it to his lips.

"Thank you."

"You're welcome."

The politeness of the exchange reminded her that they were strangers, that she knew nothing about this man who claimed to be her father.

He tried to sit up, dropped back against the pillows, visibly weakened by the effort. "You must want an explanation."

"I can't deny that. But not now."

"If not now—" He broke off there, his gaze fixed on some point outside the window, far away.

Willa sat on the edge of her chair, her hands clasped tightly in her lap. She wanted to hear, and yet not. There was safety in remaining oblivious. But it was too late for that. The box had been opened. She wanted to know.

"Your mother and I…we met one weekend when I was on the way back from Virginia," he said, his voice distant with memory. "I had gone up to see some horses in Middleburg, Virginia, and stopped on the way back at your mother's diner for dinner. We started talking, and I don't know, we just hit it off. I was quite a bit older than she was. Tanya was…a captivating woman."

Willa let the words sink in, seeing her mother through his eyes, remembering her young: thick blond hair, green eyes, pretty. "Then why—"

"Didn't something more come of it?"

She nodded.

Several moments passed before he said, "I was engaged to Natalie."

A sharp shaft of disappointment sliced through

her. She wasn't sure if it was for herself or for her mother. "That makes it all pretty terrible, doesn't it?"

He looked at her then, his eyes clouded with emotion, primary among them, guilt and grief. "I know there's no possible way you could understand. I don't expect you to. It's just that sometimes we make choices that end up hurting others when that was never our intention. When your mother told me she was pregnant, I panicked. If there's a checklist of wrong responses, I'm sure I made every one of them."

"So what happened?" Willa asked, her voice little more than a whisper now.

"I married Natalie. And by the time I came back to offer your mother help with you, she didn't want anything to do with me."

The admission surprised her. Her mother had struggled, and there had been months when the bills far outweighed the balance in her bank account. Willa stood, went to the window, her back to the bed.

"You have every right to be angry, Willa."

"It seems a little late for any of that," she said, unable to keep the edge from her voice. "I don't understand how you could go all those years knowing about me and—"

"I'm sorry," he said. "So sorry."

The words were heartfelt, and she had no doubt that he meant them now. Willa turned to look at him. "That doesn't really change anything though, does it?"

Something like pain flashed across his face, and for a moment she regretted the sharpness of her words. "No," he said. "It doesn't."

She folded her arms across her chest, suddenly cold. "Maybe we should leave it at that."

"Willa—"

"I'm sorry, but I have to go," she said and walked quickly from the room.

WILLA FOUND OWEN SITTING in the waiting room with Natalie Hartmore.

At the sight of her, they both stood.

The older woman stared at her for a long moment, her eyes dark with emotion. She looked away then and headed across the hall to her husband's room.

"Hey," Owen said, touching a hand to Willa's shoulder. "Are you all right?"

She nodded. "I understand why she hates me."

"She doesn't hate you. She's just…she's had a hard time accepting—"

"Who could blame her?" Willa interrupted.

Owen was quiet for a moment, and then said

"You look like you could use some coffee. There's a Starbucks just down the street."

"Coffee would be great," she said.

They walked the short distance without talking, ordered, then sat at a table by the window, sipping, the silence between them now growing heavy with awkwardness.

"Do you want to talk about it?" Owen asked, setting his cup on the table.

Willa released a sigh. "It's crazy. After all this time, why couldn't he just let things be? Why would a man wait until he's near the end of his life to drop this on his wife? Or to find a daughter he obviously cared nothing about?"

Owen held her gaze for several moments, as if searching for an answer that would settle more softly. "Maybe because deep down, we think there's always tomorrow. That we can count on another day. Maybe that's how we get by with putting off the hard stuff."

She took a sip of her coffee, met his gaze over the rim of her cup, weighed the words. They had certainly been true of her own life. Of the future she had given up.

"If I were you, I'd be mad as hell," Owen said.

She set the cup down. "So what if I am? What good does it do?"

"Gets you to the next emotion?"

"And what's that supposed to be?"

"I guess that's for you to decide." He reached across the table, put his hand over hers. Her fingers warmed beneath his, the touch welcome. "People make mistakes. I know it was never his deliberate intention to hurt anyone."

"But he did."

"Yeah. He did."

She was quiet for a moment, and then said, "He's not going to get better, is he?"

Owen squeezed her hand once, his expression somber. "I don't know."

She sat for a few moments, then pulled her hand away and reached for her purse. "Let's go back," she said.

THE HALLWAY OUTSIDE the bedroom Katie had been given was wide enough to drive a tractor trailer through. The walls had been done in some kind of muted Italian-looking finish, and there were lights with shades on them spaced every twelve feet or so.

She tiptoed across the dark wood floor, reached the top of the steps, and then descended to the open foyer, flip-flops flapping. A very big man with salt-and-pepper hair sat in a ladder-back chair just short of the door, reading a newspaper. His face held the lines of a life lived outdoors, his hands against the newsprint strong and capable. He lowered the paper, looked at her and said, "You must be Katie."

"Yeah. Who are you?"

"Jake. Austin."

"You always read your paper by the front door?"

He smiled, obviously ignoring the sarcasm beneath her question. "Only when I'm asked to watch out for wayward teenagers trying to leave the premises."

"A comedian, too."

His grin widened, his expression agreeable. "Now, listen, miss. The way I see it, this isn't such a bad place to hang out. I don't care to get in the middle of whatever you did, but I am going to make sure you're still here when Owen and your sister get back. So go on now, and make yourself at home. Kitchen's that way," he said, pointing. "Louisa'll fix you up somethin' good."

Katie considered arguing. She was really pretty adept at it. But something told her he probably wasn't the one she ought to try to get around. So she smiled her sweetest smile and said, "That sounds good. I think I will."

She walked through the foyer toward the kitchen. She could have found it with her nose. The delicious smell of baking bread filled the house and made her mouth water. An enormous living room sat to her left. The room had three sofas and a half dozen leather chairs angled in between. A stone fireplace took up one end of the room. Family pictures, mostly people with horses, decorated the walls.

Just ahead on the right was another room. The door was open. She stuck her head inside. A young guy, somewhere close to her age—maybe a little older—sat behind a big wooden desk, a computer in front of him. She half raised a hand and said, "Sorry."

"Hey, no problem." He waved her forward. "Come on in."

She tipped her head to the side. "I was looking for the kitchen."

"Nearly there. You have to tell me your name first, though."

He had laughing eyes. Blue as she'd ever seen. He reminded her of a young—what was that actor's name—Matthew McConaughey? His shoulders were wide, muscles apparent beneath a light blue shirt. She finally found her voice and said, "Katie Addison."

"So you're the prisoner Jake told me about."

"Hardly," she said, a blush heating her cheeks.

"Detainee, then."

"Temporary. And you are?"

"Cline Miller. Owen's brother."

"You look alike. Except your hair is lighter."

"And I'm better looking."

She smiled. "And modest, too."

He folded his arms across his chest. "So what'd you do?"

She rubbed her left elbow, hesitating. "I think I'll keep that a secret."

"Even if I promise not to tell anybody?"

"Even if." She held his amused gaze and felt something flicker inside her.

"That's a shame. I bet it's interesting. Whatever you did."

Boys had never been an issue with Katie. Flirting came as naturally as breathing. But all of a sudden, she felt gawky and awkward, and her palms were damp. She stepped a little closer to the desk. "What's so interesting on that computer?"

"Lots of stuff," he said.

"You don't look like the computer type."

"Oh, yeah? What type do I look like?"

"I'm hoping the type that might know how to get me out of this house." Okay, so she did have a few ounces of flirtation left in her. She smiled, starting to enjoy herself. She moved around the corner of the desk. "Show me what's so interesting."

He sat back, and a glint of metal caught her eye. She looked down. A wheelchair. He was sitting in a wheelchair. Shock rippled through her. She stepped away, nearly tripping over a stack of books tucked beside the desk.

She stared at him for a moment, completely at a loss for words. He couldn't be…a young guy like him? "You're—"

"Yeah," he said, his chin lifting a fraction. "I am."

"I'm sorry," she said. "I didn't know."

"Is there any reason why you should have?"

"No." She shook her head. "I just—"

His smile wasn't quite as bright when he said, "The kitchen. Take a right out of here. You'll run right into it. Tell Louisa I suggested you try some apple butter with that bread she's baking."

Katie backed up, one hand to her chest. "Thanks," she said. "I will." And with that, she turned and fled from the room.

CHAPTER SEVEN

HE TOLD HIMSELF it didn't bother him.

Cline had long ago pegged the two basic reactions girls had to his useless legs. Run like hell. Or fall all over him with motherly goodwill.

Of the two, he preferred Katie's reaction.

At least it was honest.

For a few minutes there, he'd felt like a normal guy. Understood what it would be like to meet someone cute and feel a zing of attraction. Know that it was returned without any assessment of his handicap.

Of course, he'd realized right away that she hadn't noticed the wheelchair. But it had been nice to have a girl look at him, just him, without seeing all the blaring warning signs surrounding him: Beware! Invalid ahead! Sign on for a lifetime of caretaking!

Most days, Cline did not feel sorry for himself. Even with his paralyzed legs, he managed to have a stimulating life. Once he'd finally decided to get over the self-pity, he'd realized there were things he could do, things he could be. But it wasn't ever going to be the same as his old life. And there was one truth he couldn't deny. Girls like Katie weren't interested in a guy like him. That was a cold, hard fact.

He looked at the computer screen, and with a few swift keystrokes, clicked out of the page he'd been working on.

People were people. They couldn't help themselves.

WILLA OPENED THE DOOR to the hospital room and stuck her head inside.

Charles lay against the stark white pillows. His eyes were closed.

Mrs. Hartmore sat in the chair by the window, a magazine on her lap. She glanced up at Willa, her lips thinning. "What are you doing here?"

"I wondered if it would be all right if I spoke with him once more."

"He's sleeping," she said with restrained impatience. "And I don't think it's appropriate for you to barge in here anytime you feel like it."

"Natalie." Charles was awake now, his gaze locked with that of his wife. "Please, dear."

"You need your rest," she implored.

"And I will get it. I'd like a few minutes with Willa first."

Mrs. Hartmore raised her chin, settled a level glare on Willa, then left the room, shoulders stiff.

"I'm sorry," Willa said once the door had closed.

"Don't be. Natalie—"

"You don't have to explain."

He closed his eyes for a moment, as if waiting for a wave of pain to pass.

"Are you all right?"

"Yes," he said.

"I can come back later."

"Please. Stay for a bit."

"I don't know what to say," she said. "This… everything is—"

"I know. You don't have to say anything, my dear. I just want you to believe how much I regret not knowing you. If I could change anything in the way I've lived my life, it would be that."

"We should talk about this when you're better. You really should rest," she said.

His eyes grew heavier. She stepped toward the bed, stood for a moment. His right hand lay palm up, his fingers splayed. She reached out and placed her own hand on his.

He turned it over, intertwined their fingers, holding on tight. His grip went suddenly lax. The machine beside his bed sounded an alarm. Willa jerked her hand back.

Footsteps echoed in the hall. A nurse pushed open the door, called out for assistance, then rushed to the bed.

"You'll have to excuse me, miss," she said.

Willa stepped away, heart pounding. A doctor and two more nurses ran into the room, pushing carts, throwing out orders.

Mrs. Hartmore appeared in the doorway, her expression frozen in shock. "My God. What did you say to him?"

"He was fine," Willa said, a tremble in her voice. "He closed his eyes and then he just—"

"I want you out of here!" Natalie screamed. "This is all your fault. You never should have come here!"

Owen stepped up behind Natalie, a hand on the woman's shoulder. He glanced at the bed where the doctor and nurses worked in frantic synchronicity over Charles. "What is it? What's wrong?"

One of the nurses moved away from the bed. "Could you all please wait outside?"

Mrs. Hartmore turned and walked out.

Owen took Willa's arm and led her from the room.

In the hallway, she stood with her back against the wall, her whole body throbbing with a quiet hurt that did not seem reasonable considering she had not even known of her father's existence mere days ago.

The three of them stood like statues, Mrs. Hartmore staring at her clasped hands.

And then a sudden quiet erupted from the room's open door.

"That's it. Call it," a male voice said in resigned tones.

Mrs. Hartmore turned her face into Owen's shoulder, her slim body now shaking with heavy sobs.

Willa's chest felt too tight, as if she couldn't breathe. She turned and walked toward the elevator, her steps quickening until she was running.

OWEN FOUND HER in the small park outside the hospital. He'd stayed with Natalie until her sister had arrived and then he'd left in search of Willa.

She sat on a bench just ahead, her back straight. He stopped behind her. "Hey," he said.

"Hi," she responded without looking at him.

"I was getting a little concerned about you."

"I'm fine."

He walked around the bench and sat down beside her. He didn't say anything for a few moments, his own grief a knot in his throat. "I'm so sorry," he said finally.

She started to speak, closed her mouth and

then said, "I feel this incredible sadness. And yet, it doesn't seem like I have a right to it. I didn't know him."

He turned her face to him. "Of course you have a right. I wish things had been different, that you'd had some time together. But that wasn't to be. I think he must have known that. And you're entitled to feel sad about it."

Her green eyes welled with tears. He brushed them away with a thumb. They looked at each other for a few long moments, caught in a swirl of mixed emotions. Primary among his was a sudden desire to kiss her, wipe away the shock on her face, merge his own grief with hers.

Inappropriate. For a dozen different reasons. And so, instead, he pulled her against him and rubbed her shoulder, offering sympathy as a new friend would.

AN HOUR LATER, Willa sat submerged in a warm bath. She closed her eyes and rested her head against the back of the tub, every muscle weighted with fatigue.

Sam lay on the rug just inside the room, head on his paws, asleep.

Once they'd arrived back at the farm, Owen had directed her to the room where she had left her stuff earlier, suggesting that she relax for a while against her protests that she needed to talk to Katie. He had promised to check on her sister.

Everything that had happened last night now seemed a thousand years ago. She felt numb. How could so much take place in such a short time?

In less than twenty-four hours, she'd learned of a father she had not known existed, met him and lost him. The twist of that seemed impossibly cruel. And yet, even with sadness pressing against her chest, she could not regret coming here.

As far as the future was concerned, it changed nothing. But at least she knew. At least they'd had those few minutes together.

There was no reason for her to stay any longer. She knew what kind of a reminder she must be to Natalie Hartmore. For everyone concerned, she would go.

AFTER HER BATH, Willa got dressed. As much as she would have liked to climb in the four-poster bed and sleep a solid eight hours, she needed to find Katie. They had a lot to talk about. At the very least, Willa owed her an explanation.

She knocked at the bedroom door where they'd left Katie earlier that morning. When there was no answer, she turned the knob, but the room was empty. With Sam at her heels, she went downstairs and poked her head inside a few doorways until she found Owen in a study off the main living room. What looked like a stack of work sat on the desk in front of him. She rapped lightly at the half-open door.

He looked up, then stood. "Come in."

"Sorry to bother you," she said, clasping her arms across her chest.

"No bother. Feel better?"

She nodded. "The bath helped."

"Good."

The silence between them felt awkward, as if they'd reached a new turning point, and neither had any idea what to say to each other. He looked freshly showered, his dark hair wet, his face clean-shaven. "I was looking for Katie," she said. "And I wanted to tell you we'll be leaving right away. I can rent a car so you don't have to drive us back."

He stepped out from behind the desk. "But what about the funeral?"

She linked her hands together. "I don't think it would be such a good idea for me to be there."

He moved across the floor, stopping close enough that she could smell the faint lemony scent of his aftershave. "Why?"

"I don't want to make Mrs. Hartmore any more uncomfortable than she already has been."

"Willa, you have every right to be at that funeral," he said in a quiet, convincing tone.

She shook her head. "Maybe it would be better to just let this go."

"Is that what you really want?"

She glanced down, unable to meet his discerning gaze. Was it? The truth? No. She wanted to know more about this man who had been her father. What his life had been like. Who he was. She felt as if she'd been given this incredible gift, and just as she began to let herself believe it might be real, it had been yanked away.

"Charles has asked for your place in his life to be recognized," Owen said. "Natalie will respect that."

Willa stood, running a hand up one arm. "I need some time to think. And I need to talk to Katie. Do you know where she is?"

"She went with Jake to the barn. I'll walk you down."

"If you don't mind, I'd like to talk to her by myself."

He nodded. "But at least stay tonight. Sleep on it."

That much she could agree to. And maybe a good night's rest would help her to see things more clearly. "Okay."

"Good," he said. "Dinner's at seven."

"Thanks. I'll see you then."

OWEN HAD JUST heard the front door close behind Willa when Cline rolled into the room.

He stopped short of the desk and said, "Filling our house up with good-looking women. That's a change for the better."

Owen raised an eyebrow at his brother. "You met them then?"

"Katie. Haven't met the sister yet."

"So what did you think?"

"Other than the fact that she's looking for somebody to be mad at?" he asked, wheeling across the floor to pull a book off the shelf by the window. He appeared immediately engrossed in the title.

"Cute, though," Owen said.

"Yeah." With indifference.

"I have a feeling she could use a friend."

Cline looked up then. "So what's her story?"

"Kind of a bad news boyfriend."

He flipped through the book on his lap. "Afraid I can't do much for her in that department."

"Cline—"

He held up a hand. "That wasn't a cry for help, big brother."

An old knot formed in Owen's gut. There was so much he wanted to say, but he forced himself to offer only, "You're almost eighteen, Cline. You should be dating."

Cline put the book back and turned his chair toward the door. "I'm focused on other things right now. Like making grades. You should be happy I'm not giving you gray hair with my need to rebel."

He was right. Cline was a good kid. But Owen feared that he had talked himself into settling for a life that did not include girls. "At your age, there should be more," he said quietly.

"I am a little bit of an exception though, aren't I?" And with that, he took off.

THE BARN WAS INCREDIBLE. Thirty stalls or more, and long as a football field. The exterior was white with open Dutch doors over which horses hung their heads, looking out across the fields.

Willa stepped inside the big center-aisle doors, the sweet smell of hay filling her nostrils. Sam trotted off on a scent, tail wagging. Horses moved restlessly in their stalls, a chorus of nickers sounding out.

She found Katie inside what looked like a feed room, filling red buckets with scoops of grain. "Hey," she said.

"Hi," Katie replied without looking up.

"It looks like someone put you to work."

"Beats being bored out of my skull."

Willa watched for a moment, impressed by the

careful precision with which her sister measured out the amounts. When was the last time she'd seen Katie act like she cared about anything? "I guess you're wondering what this is all about."

"The question crossed my mind." Sarcasm coated the words.

Willa sat down on a stack of red Purina feed bags, elbows on her knees. "Owen came to Pigeon Hollow to find me. At the request of—"

Katie looked at her, for once not hiding her curiosity behind a mask of rebellion. "Yeah?"

Willa glanced down at her hands, linked her fingers together, then met her sister's questioning gaze. "My father."

"What?" Katie's eyes widened. She dropped the feed scoop and wiped her hands on her jeans.

"I know. It's pretty shocking."

"How—who is he?"

"His name is Charles Hartmore." Willa drew in a deep breath. "Was."

"What do you mean, was?"

She didn't answer for a few moments, the words sticking in her throat. "He died this morning," she said softly.

Again, Katie looked as if she had no idea what to say. "Man. That's a drag."

"Yeah," Willa said, rubbing her arms, feeling suddenly cold. "It is."

They said nothing for a few moments. Outside the room, a radio played a country tune. A cat meowed.

"So what about what Mom said?" Katie shook her head. "That your dad was dead?"

"I don't know. But this man…Charles…had no reason to lie."

"And Mom did?"

"I don't know."

"Well, it is kind of weird, don't you think? She made sure I knew all about my father. What a lousy creep he was, anyway."

"Katie—"

"Don't deny it, Willa. You know it's true."

Willa pressed her lips together. The truth was their mother had said way too much about Katie's father, made way too many comparisons between him and her daughter. So many that at some point, Katie had begun to put up protective barriers around herself, and they were still in place today.

"So is he rich like our friend Owen?"

Willa frowned. "Does it matter?"

"Of course it matters. Maybe your Prince Charming finally rode in to town. Isn't that what you've been waiting your whole life for? Someone to rescue you?"

Willa flinched beneath the slap of her sister's words. "Do you intend to be as cruel as you are, Katie?"

A shadow of regret flashed across the younger girl's face, then quickly disappeared. "Sometimes the truth is cruel. You had all these plans for your life, Willa. You wanted to be a doctor. And what have you been doing? Focusing so hard on running my life that you don't have to look at your own."

"I'm not unhappy, Katie."

Katie waved a hand. "Right. You've had approximately three dates in the last how many years?"

Heat flooded Willa's face. "Where you're concerned, Katie, I've done what I wanted to do."

"You did what you thought you needed to do." Katie turned her back, filling another bucket. "I hate that you feel sorry for me."

Willa reached out and put a hand on her sister's shoulder. "Why would you say that?"

Katie stepped away from her touch. "Because Mama wished I'd never been born, and you know that."

Willa closed her eyes, bit her lip. And then in a soft voice, "Katie, Mama said a lot of things I know she never meant."

"Yeah, well. Some of them were hard to forget. And she can't exactly take them back, can she?"

How many times had Willa wished she could erase all the things their mother had said? Rewrite some of the ugly comments she had made to Katie when her grades weren't as good as Willa's or she didn't learn to ride her bike as quickly as Willa had.

But she couldn't take them back, couldn't erase them. And she feared that Katie was going to let her hurt direct the rest of her life.

"What happened last night," Willa said, "I never intended for it to turn out like that."

Katie kept her gaze on the feed scoop, dipping and dumping in an even rhythm. "What makes you so sure you know what's right for me, Willa?"

"I *don't* know, Katie," she said. "I'm just trying to prevent you from making a mistake there's every chance you're going to regret."

Katie looked up, her expression set. "I'm not going back home with you, Willa."

"You have to go back to school—"

"I'm going back to Pigeon Hollow. But I'm not going home. And I'm not going back to school."

Willa stared at her sister, saw the determination in her eyes and felt the pull of frustration in her own inability to reach her. "Katie! Eddie shot at us last night. He could have hit—"

Katie dropped the scoop, glaring at her. "If you and Owen whoever-he-is hadn't kidnapped me in the middle of the night, none of that would have happened!"

"Is that really how you see it?"

"I'm old enough to make my own decisions. You're off the hook, Willa! I don't want your help!"

The feed-room door opened. Jake, the man Owen had briefly introduced Willa to earlier, stuck his head inside, nodded at Willa and then looked at Katie. "You about done with those?"

"Just a couple more."

"I got some hungry horses out here."

Katie nodded.

Jake came in, picked up a half-dozen buckets, then disappeared out into the aisle.

Willa put a hand to her forehead and pushed her hair away from her face. "We're going to be staying a little while," she said suddenly. "I'm not sure how long."

Katie didn't look up from her task. Made no response whatsoever except for the stiffening of her shoulders.

"Owen said dinner is at seven," Willa said and walked out the door.

SHE WENT BACK TO HER ROOM, not passing anyone in the house as she went. She pulled a few items of clothing from her suitcase and took them over to the room where Katie was staying. Back in her own room, she dropped onto the bed, suddenly exhausted.

Sam curled up on a corner of the Oriental rug, nose to tail, and closed his eyes.

She reached for the phone on the nightstand, dialed the diner number. Judy answered.

"How is everything?" Willa asked.

"Everything's fine here," she said. "What's going on with you?"

Willa stretched out on the bed, staring at the ceiling. "I'm not sure where to start."

"Did you meet him?"

"Yeah, I—" The words caught in her throat, and she couldn't answer.

"What is it, honey?"

"He…died this morning." Tears slipped down her face. She wiped them away with the back of her hand.

"Willa. Dear heaven. I'm so sorry."

She rubbed her eyes. "Funny how things work out, huh?"

Judy was silent for a moment, and then said, "At least you did get to see him. I'm so glad you went."

"So am I," Willa admitted, realizing suddenly that it was true.

"How's Katie?"

"That's another issue altogether," she said on a sigh. "I think it might be good to keep her away a little longer. This whole thing with Eddie has gotten out of hand. Maybe a few days here will give her time to clear her head."

"Don't worry about the diner. I'll take care of the place."

"I owe you so big, Judy. Thank you."

"Don't mention it."

"I'll call soon."

"Bye, hon."

Willa clicked off the phone, then dialed information for Principal Keating's home number. When the answering machine picked up, she left a message telling him that she had taken Katie with her on an unexpected trip out of town. She also told him briefly about Katie's refusal to return to school, and that she was hoping some time away would help her see what a mistake that would be. She would call again to talk about the possibility of Katie's attending summer school to make up what she would miss.

Willa hung up then, closed her eyes and wondered again how so much could have happened in such a short time. Katie, Owen, her father.

Owen. He had been unbelievably kind to her today. Granted, he'd been close to Charles, and no doubt felt obligated to steer her through this. Had she imagined the connection between them? And last night when he'd kissed her...

She closed her eyes, settled on the memory and let it slide her into sleep.

CHAPTER EIGHT

WILLA WOKE JUST BEFORE SIX that evening, although she could have slept through until morning, but forced herself to get up and take a shower. It helped, and she felt awake enough to function.

She put on a sleeveless dress, light blue with a scooped neck, pulled her hair back in a ponytail and dusted some face powder over the shine on her nose. Pink lipstick. Done.

She left Sam snoring softly on the rug in her room, then knocked at the door across the hall. When Katie didn't answer, she went downstairs.

Voices drifted out from the main living room. Owen and her sister stood by the stone fireplace, talking. Katie was smiling.

Willa stood there for a moment, too off-balance to know what to say.

Owen waved her forward. "What can I get you to drink? Katie's having iced tea. I'm having a little red wine. Would you like some?"

"That would be nice," she said.

Katie's smile disappeared, and in its place settled the sullenness that had become her hallmark expression.

"I was just telling your sister about some of my escapades as a teenager and some of the chores Jake came up with to occupy my mind as he liked to put it."

"Like what?" Willa asked.

Owen picked up the wine bottle from a table on which sat glasses and a small bowl of cashew nuts. "Let's see, there was the time I turned the tractor over because I floored it going through a big mud puddle. I didn't realize there was a hole in the middle of it. Left a heck of a dent in the front end, not to mention I could have killed myself."

Willa glanced at Katie who was looking at Owen as if he'd suddenly transformed into the current MTV sensation.

"That's a little hard to picture," Willa said.

A handsome young man in a wheelchair appeared at the entrance to the room. He wore a white T-shirt that read Dave Matthews Band, Nissan Pavilion. "So this is where the party is," he said.

Owen smiled. "Willa, you haven't met my brother, Cline."

"Hi, Cline," she said, stepping forward and sticking out her hand.

"The other pretty sister."

Willa glanced at Katie, startled to see her blushing. She looked back at Cline and said, "I see this family didn't run short on charm."

Louisa stepped into the room behind him and waved a hand. "Dinner is ready."

"Thank you, Louisa," Owen said.

They followed her to the dining room where an incredible spread of food had been laid out on the buffet against one wall. An enormous terra-cotta bowl held a salad made up of baby lettuce, walnuts and roasted pears tossed in an olive oil and balsamic vinegar dressing. Another oversize dish held hot-from-the-oven lasagna, slightly browned cheese bubbling on top. A basket of warm bread sat to the side. The competing smells of yeast and garlic made Willa suddenly weak with hunger.

"We're in for a treat," Owen said. "Louisa, I see you've made Cline's favorite."

The dark-haired woman laughed a pleased laugh. "His true favorite would be a hamburger and French fries, but I try to do a little better by him than that."

Cline smiled and said, "You could cook old tennis shoes, and they'd taste good."

Louisa all but beamed, then dropped a kiss on Cline's head on the way out of the room. "Flattery, flattery. That'll keep the chocolate-chip cookies coming."

They filled their plates and moved to the table. Owen held a chair for Willa and Katie.

"There's one of the drawbacks about being in a wheelchair," Cline said. "Dad taught us the same manners. I just have a little more trouble implementing them."

Willa noted the flash of surprise in Owen's eyes.

The remark cast a net of discomfort across the remainder of the meal. They ate in relative silence.

When she finished, Willa put a hand to her stomach. "That was so good."

"I'm sure there's some dessert around here somewhere," Owen said. "Would you like some?"

"No room," she said, shaking her head.

"How about a walk then?"

"That sounds nice. I'll get Sam. He'll need to go out." And then, to Katie, "I'll be back in a little while."

"Don't worry," Katie said. "I'm not planning an escape. For tonight, anyway."

Willa went upstairs and let an ecstatic Sam out of the bedroom.

Owen stood outside the house, waiting for them. "I'm sorry about dinner," he said. "Cline isn't normally one for sarcasm. I'm not sure what's going on with him."

A three-quarter moon hung in the sky, draping the evening in light. Sam trotted off, tail wagging.

"He's in heaven here. Too many good smells."

"Horse manure, plenty of rabbits, a squirrel or two. Pretty good setup for a dog."

"I noticed you don't have one."

"Yeah," he said, blowing out a whoosh of air. "I lost mine about six months ago. A chocolate Lab I'd had for fourteen years." He was quiet for a moment. "It still hurts to think about him. Maybe I'll get another one someday. But not yet."

The words were etched with a barely concealed sadness, and Willa felt as if she'd just glimpsed some part of him he didn't often let others see. "I'm sorry," she said. "I can't imagine losing Sam. There's something about losing a dog—"

"Yeah, I know. Dogs love in a different way, don't they? Heart and soul." Silence, and then he said, "Sam doesn't seem quite as worried about me now."

"I think he's decided you're okay."

"My shin thanks him."

Willa smiled. "Did you grow up here?"

"I did," he said.

She glanced out at the bold lines of white fencing, at the enormous old oak tree to the right of the barn. "I can't imagine being able to look at this every day."

"I do love it. Growing up, it was just home. When I moved to New York City for college, I realized how much I didn't want to stay away forever. I was sort of like a cowboy boot in a store full of handmade Italian loafers. Never really fit in."

They walked down a gravel lane that ran between two pastures. To their right, a group of young horses grazed. They raised their heads and trotted to the fence. Owen stopped, leaned against the top fence board, reached out and stroked the neck of the closest one.

"How old are they?" Willa asked.

"Yearlings. All fillies here."

"How does this work?"

"We're a commercial breeder. We breed to sell at auctions like Keeneland."

She put her elbows on the fence. "Did this start with your father?"

"Grandfather."

"How do you determine which mare to breed to which stallion?"

"Horses with speed tend to pass the trait along to their offspring. You try to match the best with the best."

"It must be interesting to see how they come along."

"It is."

"They're beautiful animals."

"With incredibly big hearts."

She turned her head to look at him. "You love what you do."

"For the most part. Like any industry, there are things I'd like to see changed."

"Such as?"

"Up the starting age for racing. Give the horses more time to develop."

"Think it ever will?"

"Sad fact? Probably not."

Willa reached out to rub the muzzle of the young horse closest to her. She heard the sincerity in his voice again, liked what it said about him. "If it's all right with you, I think we'll stay a few days."

"It's more than all right."

"Thank you," she said. "For your generosity. For everything."

"There's no need to thank me. I'm really sorry about what happened today."

"At least I had the chance to meet him. You were right about that. I'm glad I came."

"Good," he said on what sounded like a note of relief. "I thought you might regret it with the way things turned out."

"No," she said. "The opposite."

They stood there, shoulder to shoulder, nearly

touching. They were silent for a while, just watching the young fillies graze, a passing cloud dimming the moonlight across the green field.

"I talked to Katie a bit before you came down," he said finally.

Willa stared at her feet. "She was actually smiling when I walked in the room."

"She seems like a good kid."

"Underneath all that rebellion, she is." Willa turned around, her back against the fence, looking toward the house. "When she was a little girl, she was the sweetest child. She always had a smile for everyone, and she thought I—"

"Walked on water?"

"Pretty much."

"Hurts like heck when that changes, doesn't it?"

"Yeah. It doesn't have to be like that again. I just wish I could get through to her somehow."

"Maybe being here will take some of the pressure off you. Give her a chance to see things with new eyes."

"At the least, it'll keep her away from Eddie for a while." She dropped her head back. "I can't even stand to think about her going back to that place with him."

"Do you think she really would?"

"Right now, yes."

"One day, she'll thank you for getting her out of there."

Willa stared at her feet. "Hard to believe that. And besides, I should be thanking you."

"I didn't exactly want to see her stay there, either."

She turned and found his gaze on her face. They studied each other for a few seconds before she dropped her own gaze. "Do you mind if I ask what happened to Cline?"

Owen propped an elbow on the fence, ran a hand through his hair. "He was in a skiing accident. We were coming down for the last run of the day. He hit a patch of ice and skidded into a tree."

Just the words made Willa's stomach drop. "Oh, Owen, I'm so sorry."

"He was twelve," Owen said. "He'd been ready to quit for the day, and I asked him to go up with me for one more run."

It was impossible to miss the blame in his voice. "You don't think you're responsible for what happened, do you?"

"Maybe that's a little too simple. I guess regret is more accurate. I don't know. He's just so young. There are so many things he hasn't done."

Willa thought about the brief interchange between the two brothers earlier at dinner. Owen had his own struggles to contend with, and yet he had stepped in to help her with Katie.

"He seems like a very smart young man," she said. "I know his life isn't going to take the path it might have taken without his accident. But maybe in some ways, it will be a better path."

"Do you really believe that?" he asked.

There was no sarcasm in his voice, but genuine interest, as if he cared what she thought. "I believe God has a plan for each of us. That sometimes it doesn't intersect with the one we lay out for ourselves. But maybe in the end it gets us to a better place."

He looked at her, appreciation in his eyes. And she thought how nice that was. Really nice.

ONCE OWEN AND WILLA HAD GONE outside, Cline left the dining room, murmuring something about some studying to do. Despite the obvious lack of invitation, Katie followed him to the office where she'd stumbled across him earlier that day.

He headed straight for the computer, ignoring her. Clearly, he wasn't thrilled by her presence. She was willing to overlook it; there was every chance she would dry up and die of boredom any second.

He hit a few strokes on the keyboard, moved the mouse and clicked on something.

Katie stood in front of the desk while he continued to ignore her. "Isn't there anything fun to do around here?" she finally asked.

"Depends on what your definition of fun is," he said without taking his eyes off the computer.

"I'm open to suggestion."

He looked up at her, his blue eyes direct. "I hate to disillusion you, Katie. But your act isn't all that subtle."

She blinked, feeling the lack of compliment in the comment. "Who says it's an act?"

"You should take it on the road. You've got the badass rebellious teenager down to a pretty convincing note."

A little whirl of anger funneled up inside her. She'd known a long list of arrogant guys, but this one took the cake. She folded her arms across her chest. "So what's up with that?"

"What?" he asked, back to his pecking and clicking.

"You don't even know me, and you've already slapped a label on me and tied it up with a ribbon and bow."

He settled his gaze on her then, gave her a long look without saying anything.

She looked away, her cheeks warm. It occurred to her that she'd blushed more in this one day than she had since she was thirteen. She didn't know much about paralyzed people, but she wondered if he had normal feelings like other guys.

But then she met his eyes again, and the answer hit her square in the chest. He felt things. Without a doubt, he felt things.

She picked up a pen from the desk, punched the end of it on and off. "How exactly did you get this cocky?"

He laughed then, a roar of a laugh that under-scored the question as falling on the other side of ridiculous. "It looks like you're the one eager to slap on labels. I just don't do well with bullshit. I'd rather call it like it is. Saves a lot of time and energy."

"Convenient, too," she said.

He sat back in his chair, started to say some-thing, stopped. Then turned around and began banging on his keyboard again.

Clearly, she'd hit a chord. She left the room be-fore the urge to take it back won out.

WILLA AWOKE THE NEXT MORNING to a knock at her door. She raised up on one elbow, squinting at the clock.

Eleven. With a low moan, she pushed her hair back from her face and said, "Come in."

Owen stuck his head inside. "Good morning."

"Morning," she said, suddenly thinking what she must look like.

"Natalie called to say there will only be one service. Tomorrow afternoon at one o'clock. I thought you and Katie might like to go shopping. For something to wear."

"Thank you. That would be nice."

"You can take the Rover."

The thin strap of her pajama top slid from her shoulder. She pushed it back in place. "Thanks."

His gaze followed her hand, then lifted abruptly to her face. "Well. Okay. The keys are in it."

"Great."

Sam got up, stretched, walked to the door.

"Want me to take him out?"

"Would you mind? He's not used to sleeping this late, either."

"Sure. See you later."

Willa and Katie left the farm early that afternoon. Willa drove to an area Owen had described as having numerous stores that ranged in style and price. Katie stared out the window most of the way, silent, but without the sullenness Willa had grown to expect.

She braked at a stoplight, glanced at her sister. "What are you thinking about, Katie?"

She said nothing for a few moments, and then, "Just wondering what it must feel like to know you had a father you might hold your head up for."

The light turned green. Willa drove through the intersection, the underlying hurt in her sister's voice tightening her grip on the wheel. "Katie—"

"But then maybe he wasn't so great considering that he waited until he was dying to let you know he existed."

The words sliced deep, the cut all the sharper for the truth at their edge.

"Hey, we could make some comparisons!" Katie said. "That might be entertaining. We could call it the Tanya Addison: This Was Your Life Show." She dropped her voice an octave. "Behind curtain number one, we have Mr. Charles Hartmore. Good choice, Tanya! Whoops! Should have gotten that marriage certificate in hand first. Too bad, this one's gonna get away.

"And that leaves you with curtain number two. Oh, no, Tanya. Bad choice. You're going to get another kid out of this particular loser. One you don't want and will spend the rest of your life making sure she knows it."

The words felt like nails being pounded into Willa's heart. She swung in at a post office, pulled the Range Rover into a parking spot and shut off the engine. She turned in her seat, her voice beseeching when she said, "Mama made some mistakes, Katie, but—"

"She hated me!" Katie cried, throwing her hands in the air. "You know it's true."

Willa put her arms around her sister, pulling her close despite her resistance. Katie held herself stiffly, even as sobs erupted from her throat. "She didn't hate you," Willa said softly, a dozen bad memories forming a collage over the words.

"How about 'wished I was never born?' Would you buy that?"

Willa closed her eyes, pressed her lips together. Sounds reverberated in her head. Slamming doors. A kitchen pot hurling into the living room, hot soup splattering the walls like a bad contemporary painting. Willa and Katie running upstairs to their shared bedroom, huddling together in the dark closet while rage erupted below.

Willa, torn between helping her mama and taking care of her four-year-old sister who sat shaking in her arms.

Sometimes at night, when sleep refused to immediately pull her in, Willa could still hear the sounds in her head. Her mother's crying, Clyde's awful cursing. It had taken less than nothing to set him off, and for the four years he had lived with them, it had been like existing in a house rigged with land mines. One misstep, and life exploded into barely recognizable pieces.

Every night, Willa had prayed that he would

leave, that they could have a normal house where the walls didn't shake with one man's fury. And then one afternoon, Sheriff Brown had knocked at their door, hat in his hand, a solemn look on his face. Willa and Katie had stood in the hallway behind their mother, holding hands, the words drifting back to them as if they were being delivered through some kind of horn that distorted their sound. Clyde. Dead. He'd lost control of the dump truck he drove for a living in a curve just a few miles from the house. He wasn't coming home.

As the reality of that sank in, Willa had literally dropped to her knees with relief. Katie tucked herself inside Willa's arm, pressed her small face to her neck.

None of them had cried at his funeral.

"Mama made mistakes, Katie," Willa said now, smoothing a hand across the back of her hair.

"And I was the permanent reminder of that." She pulled away and sat back in her seat. "On a good day, she could barely stand to look at me. So don't make up some fairy tale! You're so good at that. Pretending things are something other than what they are."

"Is that how you see me?" Willa asked quietly.

"I think you've gotten comfortable with me being the yoke around your neck."

Willa sat, not knowing what to say.

"Whether you like it or not, pretty soon you're not going to have me as an excuse anymore. And then maybe you'll have to admit that what I'm saying is true." Katie stared out the window.

Willa started the engine and backed out of the parking place. They drove the rest of the way to the store in silence.

CHAPTER NINE

THE FUNERAL TOOK PLACE on Monday afternoon.

Willa had several sets of second thoughts about going, but in the end, decided it was something she had to do.

Owen and Cline drove Katie and her to the service at the Christ Our Savior Episcopal Church. It was nearly full when they walked in, and Willa felt the gazes of a half-dozen people who turned to stare as they entered. She smoothed a hand across the skirt of her simple black dress and wondered if anyone else here knew. She met the gaze of a clearly curious forty-something woman and realized that her identity was not a secret.

Owen took Willa's elbow and steered her to the second pew on the right side of the sanctuary, his touch protective in a way that fortified her resolve not to dwell on what others would think.

The service was brief, the words offered about this man who had been her father, respectful, honoring. A violinist played "Ave Maria," and Willa's throat tightened with the poignant strains. Katie sat next to her, back straight, hands crossed in her lap, face blanked of expression.

Following the service, the line of cars drove slowly from the church to the cemetery, headlights on. The procession stretched out of sight in either direction.

At the grave site, Owen pulled in behind the black town car carrying Natalie and two older women. Willa got out and walked to the tent where four rows of folding chairs had been set up on a green rug. She stood looking down at the rose-draped coffin, feeling the futility of an effort that had been too little, too late.

OWEN STOOD IN THE LIVING ROOM, talking to Charles's attorney and longtime golfing buddy, Art Travers.

Willa had excused herself a few minutes before to go to the ladies' room. Katie and Cline sat beside a table loaded with a dozen different kinds of cake and at least as many pies, looking as if they had no idea what to say to one another.

"We're really going to miss him," Art said, sincerity in his voice. "Charles was a good man."

Pamela walked up just then and put her hand on Art's arm. "He certainly knew how to leave with a good exit line, though, didn't he? In fact, it looks as if Owen has taken Charles's surprise love child under his wing. And the other sister, too. Now she doesn't belong to Charles, does she?"

"Pamela," Owen rebuked, shooting a glance at the entrance to the living room.

Pamela shrugged. "I suppose it's always possible, isn't it?"

Willa appeared in the doorway, looking uncertain, rousing all of Owen's protective instincts.

"Ah, here she is," Pamela said a few moments later.

"Willa Addison," Owen said, somehow reluctant to make the introduction, "this is Pamela Lawrence."

"Nice to meet you," Willa said.

Pamela smiled. "Likewise. Will you be staying in Lexington long?"

"I'm not sure," Willa said.

"This whole thing has to be a shock to you."

"Pamela," Owen said, "Willa must be tired."

Pamela looked at Owen, gracious. "Of course. If there's anything at all I can do, please ask."

Owen saw the surprise register in Willa's eyes just before she said, "Thank you."

Owen introduced Art to her, and they shook hands.

"I was a good friend of your...of Charles," Art said diplomatically.

Willa nodded and tried to smile.

"So Owen didn't tell me," Pamela said. "Where are you from?"

Willa looked at Pamela and said, "Pigeon Hollow."

Pamela raised an eyebrow. "How quaint."

Owen put a hand to Willa's shoulder and said, "If you'll excuse us, there's something we need to discuss."

He steered her out of the crowd and onto the terrace.

"You didn't have to do that," she said once they were outside.

"What?"

"Rescue me."

He raked a hand through his hair. "I'm sorry about all that. Pamela can be——"

"You two are…" The words trailed off in question.

"I'm not sure what we are," he said.

"Ah."

Something in her voice made him feel as if he'd just been caught cheating on a final exam. Her disapproval was tangible, and he had the distinct impression she was severely disappointed in him. "I haven't lied to you, Willa."

She leaned against the rock wall of the terrace, staring out across the green lawn. "But you haven't exactly been up-front."

"You asked if I was married. I'm not married."

"I should have been more specific then. Attached."

"I never meant to mislead you."

"Then I'm a little confused about that kiss the other night."

He drew in a deep breath, released it slowly. "Yeah, me, too."

She looked him straight in the eye. "So how do you explain that in light of your having a girlfriend?"

"I can't. All I know is it was something I very much wanted to do."

She turned her gaze back to the lawn where a sprinkler system had just turned on. "That doesn't mean it should have happened."

"Willa—"

The door behind them opened. A young woman in a black-and-white serving uniform walked out to where they stood by the balcony. "Miss Addison?"

"Yes," Willa said.

"Mrs. Hartmore has asked to see you. Would you please come with me?"

She nodded.

Owen put a hand on her arm. "We'll finish this later?"

"I think we're done," she said and followed the young woman back inside.

Owen stayed where he was, preferring the solitude to going back in and making small talk.

Pamela. He'd backed her into a corner, and he couldn't blame her for showing her claws. She was a well-liked person, and over the past year, they'd had fun together. He couldn't say it had ever been more than that. She wanted more. And if anyone had the motivation to get married, it should be him. The farm he loved was at stake. Pamela had seemed like the obvious answer.

Maybe too obvious.

"SHE'S JUST INSIDE there." The young woman who had led Willa to this room at the far end of the house smiled shyly and then left.

Willa hesitated, then knocked.

"Come in, please."

She opened the door and stepped inside. Natalie Hartmore stood by an enormous window, a teacup in her hand. She was an elegant woman, medium blond hair pulled back in a crisp chignon at the back of her neck. She wore a few pieces of expensive-looking jewelry, her black dress a perfect backdrop. Her makeup was flawless, her puffy eyes the only clue to her grief.

She moved to the serving set in the middle of a small table. "Would you like some?" she asked, her voice strained. "It's a green tea."

"Yes. Thank you."

The older woman's hand shook as she poured. Willa stepped forward and took the pot. "I can do that," she said softly.

Natalie Hartmore sat in a nearby chair, sipped from her own tea. "Please sit down."

Willa took the chair across from her, sitting on the edge, her back straight. "I haven't had a chance to tell you how sorry I am for your loss."

The other woman was quiet for a few moments, and then in a somber voice said, "And I, yours."

Willa blinked in surprise. That she had not expected. "Thank you," she said.

She rubbed her thumb across the rim of her saucer, not meeting Willa's gaze. "I knew nothing about you until after Charles had his first heart attack. I won't insult you by pretending I was anything other than heartbroken. And angry."

"Mrs. Hartmore, you don't have to justify your feelings to me," she said quietly. "I think I can understand how you must feel."

"We both know this has the potential to be an ugly situation." She pressed two fingers to the bridge of her nose, as if reaching for composure. "But there's one thing true about getting old. You learn to recognize the battles worth fighting, and the ones that really aren't battles at all. That said, I see no reason you and I should be adversaries, Willa."

Willa set her teacup on the table next to her chair. "Mrs. Hartmore. I have no intention of interfering in your life in any way. If you think that I might somehow believe I have a right to any of this," she said, waving a hand at the room where they sat, "you would be very wrong. I have no reason to doubt that Charles was my father. I can't imagine why he would lie about it. But biology alone doesn't make a relationship, and if I had ever wanted anything from him, it might have been that."

Mrs. Hartmore stared at her, silent, as if she weren't sure what to make of what she'd just heard.

Willa stood. "I know you must be tired. And I think it's time for me to go."

The older woman placed her cup on the table, folded her hands in her lap. "Can you be here at two o'clock tomorrow afternoon?"

"Why?" she asked.

"For the reading of the will."

Stunned, Willa said, "But I can't—"

"You were his daughter," she said, her voice matter-of-fact now. "It's important that you come. Please."

"Mrs. Hartmore—"

"I think it's time you called me Natalie. I'll be expecting you."

THEY HEADED BACK TO THE HOUSE just before six, Cline and Katie following behind in Cline's van.

Willa told Owen about her talk with Natalie, about the reading of the will the following day. "I don't feel right about going," she said, staring out the window.

"Why?" Owen asked, glancing at her, one hand on the wheel.

"Because we weren't a part of each other's lives. I don't even know him. I never will."

"Maybe this is his way of trying to make up for that."

They said nothing for the rest of the drive. Willa felt a new tension between them, but she had meant what she'd said out on the terrace. She just didn't have it in her to play with fire when she already knew what it felt like to get burned.

Sam greeted them at the door in full body wag.

Louisa had left a note for Owen that Jake wanted him to come to the barn when he got in. Katie said she was tired and went upstairs.

Cline looked at Willa. "It's Louisa's afternoon off. I make a mean sandwich. Care to join me?"

What she really wanted to do was settle into a hot bath, and try to absorb all that had happened that day. But he was looking at her as if he hoped she might say yes. "Just let me take Sam out first."

She returned a few minutes later to find Cline

pulling sliced turkey, provolone cheese, mayon-
naise, lettuce and tomatoes from the refrigerator.

She found a couple of plates and arranged four
pieces of the homemade bread Louisa had left on
a cherry cutting board. They worked in silence for
a few minutes, ending up with two mountainous
sandwiches over which Cline waved a hand and
said, "Now that's a work of art."

"For a party of eight," Willa said. "I think I'll
cut mine in half."

"Don't worry. I'll finish what you don't eat."

Willa passed him a half and then took a bite of
hers. "Good," she said.

"Um. I was starving."

Sam lay stretched out beside Willa's chair. She
tore off a piece of her turkey, gave him a bite. She
glanced back up to find Cline studying her.
"What?"

"You can start anytime," he said.

She wiped her mouth with a napkin, frowning.
"With?"

"The list."

"I'm afraid you've lost me."

"The tell-me-about-Owen list. I've pretty well
got it memorized by now. That's my role as little
brother, you know. To prep all potential girlfriends
on his likes and dislikes. Stuff that might trip you
up. Of course, you know he has a girlfriend. But

you're a lot prettier than she is. Possibly nicer, too."

Willa sat back in her chair, her face heating. "I think you have the wrong idea about me."

"Do I? You know about his other problem then?"

She had a feeling this was the part where she should say it was none of her business and head upstairs for that bath. That she would regret not doing so. "No," she said.

"This little stipulation our father left in his will. Majority ownership of Winding Creek Farm and all its assets went to Owen upon Dad's death. The fly in the ointment being that he has to become engaged before his thirty-third birthday. And marry within six months of that. If he doesn't, then it all goes to me."

Willa blinked, more than a little taken aback by the revelation. "Why would your father do such a thing?"

"Oh, something about not wanting his son to make the same mistakes he made."

Willa sat silent for a moment. "Why are you telling me this?"

"Maybe because with you in the picture, it all gets more interesting."

"And the same provision applies to you?"

"Nope. I guess Dad didn't think there was much chance I'd turn out to be a playboy."

The words were issued lightly, but Willa heard pain at their core. "Owen doesn't seem like the type to let that kind of decision be made for him."

"He's not. But then he's had a few years to pick someone. And time's running out."

"So maybe Pamela's the lucky girl," she said, trying for a note of indifference.

"That's what I was thinking." Half smile. "Until you came along."

Footsteps sounded in the hallway. Owen walked into the kitchen. "Got any more of that to go around?"

"Fridge is full," Cline said. He picked up his plate, rolled across the floor and stuck it in the dishwasher, then left the room, Sam trotting off behind him.

Owen washed his hands at the sink. "Was it something I said?"

Willa fiddled with her napkin. "I don't think so."

"All right if I join you?"

"Sure."

He pulled some things from the refrigerator, set them on the table and started making his own sandwich.

"Cline told me about your father's will."

Jaw set, Owen said, "Yeah, ridiculous, huh?"

"How could you let this place go?"

He sat down at the table. "It wouldn't be my first choice. Although when he died, I wasn't sure I wanted to take it over, as much as I loved it. I had my own life, my own career."

She leaned forward, put an elbow on the table. "What did you do?"

"I was an attorney for the Sunrise Foundation. It's an organization in New York City that grants wishes for poverty-stricken children."

Willa sat back in her chair. "That's amazing."

"Every summer, we have a camp here for children who've never been on a farm. This will be the third time we've had it. The first two were a big hit. We have a few older mares that are really good with the kids and don't mind being hugged on all day."

She shook her head. "That's wonderful, Owen."

"You're surprised," he said.

"A little, I admit."

"That's good, I guess. At least surprises are interesting."

They sat for a moment, silent.

"So, your father," Willa said. "Why would he put such a provision in his will?"

Owen sighed. "It might take me a while to answer that one."

She rubbed a thumb across the rim of her plate, distracted by the muscles of his arms, the well-cut ridge between bicep and tricep. "I'm not going anywhere."

Owen sat back, pushed his plate away. "He was a last-word kind of man. I remember once when I was fifteen or so, he gave me this colt whose sire had won the Derby. Beautiful horse. Fast as lightning. I was crazy about him. Which frustrated Dad to no end. He didn't believe in getting attached to the horses. To him, they were strictly business tools, and there was no place for emotion when decisions had to be made about them. Anyway, I wanted to hold him back another year, let him get a little stronger." His voice softened, regretful. "Dad insisted he had to be run as a two-year-old. Fractured his cannon bone in the last stretch."

"Oh, Owen," she said.

"Dad's assessment was that given what happened, he would never have held up. Better to prove it before we had too much invested in him."

"That seems so—"

"Harsh?"

"Yeah."

"There wasn't a lot of gray in my dad's way of thinking. Everything was pretty much black and white. Including his belief that I should marry and settle down in a way that he never did after he lost my mom."

"When did she die?"

"I was three," he said, his voice growing distant. "I don't think he ever got over it. Kind of spent the rest of his life with a revolving door where women were concerned."

"I'm sorry."

"Thanks."

Willa was quiet for a moment. "What about Cline's mother?"

"They never married. She was a lot younger and had no interest in being a mother."

"Does Cline want the farm?"

"He says no, but he's young."

"If it goes to him, can't he just sell it back to you or something?"

Owen shook his head. "My father pretty much closed up all the loopholes."

"Is the thought of marriage that bad?"

"No. But the thought of being forced to marry is."

She eyed him for a moment, then said, "And you've never met anyone you wanted to marry?"

He shook his head. "Have you?"

"What?"

"Ever wanted to get married?"

The question threw her. She dropped her gaze and said, "I didn't realize we were talking about me."

"Artful dodge," he said.

"What's so bad about Pamela?" she asked, ignoring the accusation.

"There's really nothing bad about her."

"Then what?"

He shrugged. "I don't know. I guess I'm wondering about the click thing."

"The click?"

"Yeah, that feeling you're supposed to get when you meet the right person."

"Oh," she said, nodding. "The click."

"You believe in it?"

She ran a hand through one side of her hair. "I'm sure it happens for some people. But I'm also sure some good marriages have been built on less."

"Sounds like you're trying to sell me on the idea."

"Hardly."

"It just seems a little weird for us to be having this conversation."

"Weird how?"

"A couple reasons, really."

Something in his eyes made her stomach drop

like the snap of a hinge. "Are you going to elaborate on that?"

"Okay, reason number one. I'm sitting here thinking how beautiful you are. And reason number two. I'd really like to kiss you again."

Willa tried to speak, but couldn't think of a single thing to say. If he had leaned over and followed through, she would have been hard-pressed to recall her own arguments from earlier that afternoon. It was one thing to tell yourself a man like this was trouble when you were alone and had all your walls securely in place. But sitting across from him, the honesty and attraction in his eyes were a powerful pull.

She stood, a little too quickly, her chair teetering before righting itself. She picked up her plate and glass, crossed the kitchen to the sink and put them in the dishwasher.

She turned then, and with distance as a barrier, said, "We already talked about this."

"That doesn't make it go away."

"You're not playing fair."

"I'm not playing," he said.

CHAPTER TEN

IT WAS DARK WHEN CLINE rolled his chair out of the house and down the paved drive to the barn. He'd been up in his room the past couple hours surfing the Internet when it occurred to him that he was sick of going into chat rooms where he only talked to people who had no idea who he really was.

Of course, he never told them he was paralyzed. It was the only place he could go where nobody knew, where he could be a guy who flirted with girls and no one could judge him by anything except the words he offered them. But something about it tonight made him feel like a pretend person. As if he had no idea who he was or who he might ever be.

He slid open one side of the barn's main entrance, wheeled his chair down the asphalt aisleway. The barn lights were dim, Jake already having come through for night check.

Cline stopped in front of one of the stall doors. A young filly stuck her head out and nuzzled his shoulder. "Hey," he said, pressing his face against her soft nose. She nudged him gently, and he inhaled the wonderful horse scent of her.

He would never ride again. He didn't let himself think about stuff like that often, but sometimes a yearning for something he used to do would hit him so solidly in the chest that he could barely breathe for wanting that ability back.

"What's with the long face?"

He jerked his head around. Katie stood to his right, arms folded across her chest. He gave her a glare meant to send her running. "What are you doing down here?"

"I asked you first."

"No long face," he said.

"Hm. Not what I see from here."

"Hey, you know, Katie, I'm not in the mood for your tough act tonight."

"So what's wrong?" Her voice had softened, and he caught a glimpse of who she might be underneath all that toughness.

He shook his head. "I wasn't very nice to your sister earlier. Sometimes, I'm a real jerk."

White teeth worried her bottom lip. "If anybody could justify it, it's probably you."

"People have far worse things happen to them than this."

"Yeah. It still sucks." She stepped closer,

rubbed the filly's nose, reached in her pocket and pulled out a sugar cube, which promptly disappeared. "Jake said it was all right to give them treats now and then," she said.

"So you do have a warm and fuzzy side?"

"Don't get carried away."

He smiled. "I think I already know better."

Down the aisle, a horse nickered. Another answered. They said nothing for a bit, and Cline found himself hoping she would stay.

"You have any friends?" she asked, breaking the silence.

"I'm not a complete recluse."

"No need to get prickly. I was just wondering if there was anything fun to do around here."

"Let's see, we've got putt-putt. And there's bingo over at the seniors' lodge on—"

She laughed a deep belly laugh.

He smiled, thinking what a good sound that was. And at the same time, enjoying the fact that he had given her a reason to do so.

OWEN WAS UP at dawn.

Sleep had been a wasted effort, anyway. He made a pot of coffee and despite the knots in his shoulders, forced himself to sit down at his desk and respond to some work-related e-mails he'd gotten behind on the past couple of days.

But the same thing that had kept him awake most of the night now prevented him from concentrating on the work in front of him.

What was it about Willa that suddenly had him feeling as if his life were a cage made of iron bars?

Natalie called just before seven, sounding a little more like herself this morning. They spoke for a few minutes. He had just hung up when Willa appeared in the doorway to his office, Sam at her heels. "Good morning," she said.

He stared at her for a moment. She looked fresh and pretty in a sleeveless pink blouse and white pants. "Morning," he said. "That was Natalie. She asked if I could come with you today. She said Charles's sisters would be there and that you might need reinforcement."

"You don't have to do that."

"I'd like to. How about some coffee?"

She nodded, and they went into the kitchen. She held the cups, while he poured, their movements stiff like two people who weren't exactly sure how to behave with one another.

They sat at the table. Sam stood in front of the glass-pane door, staring with yearning out at the backyard where one of the barn cats was perched on a fence post.

Owen opened the newspaper, offered Willa a section. They read for a couple of minutes, quiet.

"I thought you had to be married forty years before you could sit at a table and not talk to each other," Willa said.

He looked up and smiled. "You've noticed those people?"

"It makes you wonder if they've just decided it's all been said, and there's no point in repeating it."

He put down the paper. "If they could have seen that far into the future, do you think they would ever have gotten married?"

"Probably. It would be nice to get to the end of your life and be so certain of having picked the right path that you would be willing to do the same things all over again. Conversation lulls and all."

"It would," he agreed, holding her gaze.

Silence, and then she said, "Look, Owen, about—"

"What I said yesterday?"

"Yeah."

"Out of line, right?"

"No, it's just I'm not good with this kind of thing." She studied the table. After a few moments, she looked up at him and said, "It's been a really long time since I wanted anyone to kiss me. I'd be lying if I said I didn't want you to. But I don't believe in getting in the middle of someone else's—"

"Mess?" he finished for her.

"Life," she said softly.

"Yeah," he said. "Life."

AT NATALIE'S HOUSE, the small group attending the meeting gathered in the library. Natalie had greeted them with a gracious but sad smile, and escorted them into the room where she introduced two unsmiling white-haired women as Charles's sisters, Margaret and Harriette. They were dressed in nearly matching navy suits, one with gold buttons down the front of the jacket, the other with silver. Diamond earrings the size of well-fertilized peas comprised their only jewelry. Both gave Willa a nod that could be described at best as chilly.

A dark-haired man and woman in their fifties sat beside each other on a small sofa. Their clothes were less extraordinary, he in a modest gray suit, she in a conservative black dress. They both stood and shook Willa's hand, their smiles genuine. "We're Manuel and Maria Gonzalez. We worked for your father for twenty-five years."

Willa tried to smile, her eyes stinging at their warm acknowledgment. "It's very nice to meet you."

The older sister, Margaret, silver buttons, stepped forward then and said, "One might wonder at the timing of it all. My goodness, that he would die on the very day you meet him for the first time."

Willa blinked at the accusation underscoring the words.

Owen put a hand on her back. "I don't think that could be called anything except a tragedy."

"Yes, of course," Margaret said, obviously unconvinced.

Art Travers, the attorney Willa had met the evening before, walked into the room, an enormous briefcase in one hand. "Good afternoon, everyone. Sorry I'm late."

Natalie brought in a tray with coffee and tea, set it on the round table in the middle of the room. "Please, help yourselves," she said.

The attorney placed his things on a table that had been positioned at one end of the room. He clasped his hands together, his expression somber. "As you know, we'll be going over Charles's last will and testament this afternoon. If you could all take a seat, we'll get started."

Willa had a sudden urge to run from the room. Owen put a hand on her arm, squeezed once, as if he knew what she was thinking.

He led her to a set of club chairs next to the Gonzalezes. Margaret and Harriette sat on either side of Natalie, holding her hands.

The icy looks being sent Willa's way were enough to make their opinions of her presence here more than clear.

Art pulled an official-looking document from his briefcase, along with a DVD case. He held up both. "Charles made his last wishes known in writing as well as on video. Everything you're about to see on this DVD is documented here with the appropriate signatures and witnesses."

He opened the DVD case, pulled out the disk and placed it in the player beside a television. He pushed a button, and Charles appeared on the screen.

"Hello, my dear family," he said.

Immediately, a soft sob slipped from Natalie's throat.

Willa's chest tightened with emotion, tears springing to her eyes. He looked different here than he had in the hospital, giving her a glimpse of the healthy, vibrant man he had once been.

And it struck her then that she had inherited his eyes, their shape, color, even the thickness of his lashes.

"I know this will not be an easy time, so I would like to make it as brief as possible. Natalie, my dear, the bulk of my estate will obviously go to you. The specifics of this are accounted for in my written will. I never deserved you, sweetheart, but

I did love you, and I'm sorry for anything I did to hurt you."

Willa could not bring herself to look at Natalie, but knew the older woman was crying. She could feel the stares of the two women seated beside her.

"To my sisters Margaret and Harriette, I leave the stocks and other investments left to me by our father. I believe it's right that they should go to you."

Margaret pressed her lips together. Harriette wiped her eyes.

"To Manuel and Maria, thank you for your many years of faithfulness. I leave to you the cottage on Maple Run Farm and the five acres of land surrounding it. I also leave to you the sum of two hundred and fifty thousand dollars which I hope will express my appreciation of you and everything you did for me."

Maria gasped, and then began to cry. Manuel put his arms around her, shaking his head in disbelief.

"And to Willa..." Charles broke off there, emotion roughening his voice. Willa's heart began to thump hard, and it suddenly felt difficult to breathe. Owen reached over, took her hand.

"I have no way of knowing whether we will have actually met or not. But it is my sincere hope that we did. And that as you're watching this, you might have some understanding of how very much I wish I could go back and redo a few things in my life. One of them would be to insist to your mother that I had a right to know you. The other would be to somehow try to make up for the fact that you grew up without a father. I can't do either of those things now. But you are my daughter, and since I haven't been there for you while I was alive, maybe I can be of some help with your future. I leave to you the sum of two million dollars."

The two sisters gasped in unison, a mutual sound of outrage. Willa looked at Natalie. Her expression was blank.

Willa felt as if the world around her had been turned upside down, nothing recognizable from her current viewpoint. She needed air. Had to get out of here. "I'm sorry," she said, and fled from the room.

OWEN CAUGHT UP WITH HER outside. She leaned against the Range Rover, arms wrapped around her waist as if she were trying to hold some terrible pain inside.

"Hey," he said. "Are you all right?"

"Can we go?" she asked, looking shaken.

"Don't you want to finish in there?"

"I don't belong here."

"I think you clearly do. Willa, he wanted you to have that."

"Two million dollars. He didn't know me. How could he—"

He put a hand on her shoulder, squeezed even as he resisted the urge to pull her into his arms and give her the comfort she so obviously needed. "All I know is what little he said to me when he asked me to come and see you. He had spent a good deal of time thinking about you, and I don't know why he didn't do it sooner, but he really wished that he had."

"I can't go back in there now," she said, wrapping her arms more tightly about herself.

"You're shivering." He did pull her to him then, telling himself it was what any friend worth his salt would do.

She leaned into him, pressed her face to his chest. He could feel her tears through his shirt. He rubbed her back, and felt a tenderness for her that did not seem logical given how long they'd known each other.

But then from the moment he'd set eyes on her, there had been something different in her effect on him.

He held her until her breathing grew even, and she leaned back to look up at him. He brushed her cheeks with his thumb. "It's okay if you want to leave. I'll just go tell Natalie."

She nodded, closing her eyes for a second, and then, "Thank you."

He opened the Range Rover door, waited for her to slide inside. "I'll be right back."

CHAPTER ELEVEN

THEY HAD JUST PULLED OUT of the driveway onto the main road when Owen picked up his cell phone and punched in a number.

"Hey, Jake, it's me. Can you reschedule that sales meeting this afternoon? See if tomorrow morning will work." He paused. "Katie still with you? Good. Willa's with me. We'll be back later."

"You didn't have to do that," Willa said when he'd hung up.

"What you need is a little escape from reality. Come to think of it, I could use one myself."

Willa started to protest.

But for once, it was nice to let someone else be in charge.

They drove for a good while without talking. The county roads became more rural, more space appearing between the houses. He turned onto a small state road that led to a marina. A few trucks sat in the parking lot, boat trailers hooked behind them. Owen parked and came around for her door.

"Are you going to tell me what we're doing?" she asked.

"Not yet," he said. He took her elbow and steered her toward the marina entrance. A small store sat at one corner of the dock. Boats were moored alongside. A Seadoo sat at the gas pump, a young boy filling it up with gas.

The sign above the store door said, Welcome to Tiner's on Lake Altmore.

An older man wearing a bill cap with an open mouth bass on the front stepped out and said, "Well, look what the cat drug in. On a weekday, no doubt."

"Hey, Artis. Meet my friend Willa."

"Hello, Willa," he said, sticking out a sun-browned hand, his smile revealing bright white teeth.

"Nice to meet you," she said.

"Likewise. Owen taking you on a tour of the lake?"

"I'm not exactly sure."

Artis smiled. "Well, he picked a good day for it."

Willa looked up at the sky and then out at the glistening lake beyond the marina's no-wake buoys. The sun sat high, a few puffy white clouds the only concession to imperfection.

"Got any food in there, Artis?" Owen asked.

"You know it. Go on in. Madge'll fix you up. I need to pump some gas."

The smells inside the store were mouthwatering. A woman, fiftyish, wearing a head full of pin curls and a mumu-style housedress stood behind the counter of the grill, putting together a row of sandwiches. "Hey, Owen," she said.

"Madge. How's life treating you?"

"Can't complain. Who's this pretty girl you got with you?"

"Willa Addison. Willa, Madge Tiner."

They exchanged smiles. Madge wiped her hands on the front of the white apron tied at her ample waist. "What can I get you?"

"A picnic," Owen said. "Can you put something together for us?"

"I'd be delighted," she said.

Owen winked at her. "Thanks, Madge. We'll get the boat ready while you're doing that."

Madge smiled at Willa, giving her a look every woman instantly understands. *He's something, isn't he?*

Outside, they followed the walkway to the far end of the dock. A row of boats sat parked there, the closest one a long red number, the kind that when wound out sounded as if it had a jet engine under its hood.

Next to it was a pontoon-style houseboat. Owen passed the speedboat and stepped onto the pontoon.

Willa stopped, eyebrows raised. "The speedboat's not yours?"

Owen looked back and grinned at her. "You persist in those stereotypes. I'm getting a lot of enjoyment out of proving you wrong about me."

She smiled, couldn't help herself. "Have to admit. Not what I expected."

"I call it my thinking boat. Anytime I've got something to work out, this is where I come."

Across the cove, a young boy threw a Frisbee into the water. An exuberant yellow Lab barked and sailed off the dock after it. A neon-orange Seadoo steered around the swimming Lab.

"It's great," she said.

"Step aboard. Make yourself at home."

Willa looked around while Owen got everything untied and opened up. The cabin was spacious with a sofa and two club chairs.

Tucked into a corner, a bookshelf held a collection of hardcover novels. She climbed a set of stairs that led to the upper deck. Two yellow-and-white lounge chairs beckoned. She sat down in one, leaned her head back and closed her eyes. The warm sun felt glorious. Within a few minutes, the engine started, and they began to pull away from the marina. The boat idled toward open water, and as soon as they passed the no-wake buoys, eased into full throttle.

The lake was beautiful, the water a dense blue-green. Big, expensive houses lined the shores, and then began to thin out, until the waterfront consisted only of pastureland with cows grazing on green grass. The boat began to slow until they were idling into the back of a cove. The engine shut off, and there was a splash of something that sounded like an anchor hitting the water.

A few moments later, Owen appeared at the top of the stairs. "My favorite spot," he said, sitting in the chair beside her.

"It's so peaceful."

"I know."

They sat for a while, faces tipped to the sun, absorbing the calm. The stress of the morning drained out of her, as if an internal plug had been pulled.

"I've got a change of clothes downstairs. Bathing suits are in the closet off the bathroom if you'd like to try one."

She looked down at the pantsuit she'd worn that morning, started to say she was fine, and then changed her mind. Why not?

Owen showed her where to go and then left her to sort through the half-dozen swimsuits, most with the tags still on. She chose a modest one-piece, black with a matching, short tie-around skirt.

Barefoot, she padded back out to the front of the boat where Owen had already changed into a pair of stylishly baggy swimming trunks and a white T-shirt.

He looked at her and said, "Wow."

A blush heated her face. "I won't even ask the reason for your department-store selection."

He had the grace to look chagrined. "No one's ever looked that good in any of them."

He picked up a couple of white paper bags from one of the boat seats. "Hungry?"

"Starving," she said.

They climbed the stairs to the upper deck. Owen spread out a quilt, and then began pulling food from the bags. They ate turkey sandwiches on thick slices of homemade wheat bread with bright red tomatoes and Swiss cheese. Drank iced lemonade with fresh slices of lemon floating on top. The finale, two enormous slices of coconut-cream pie.

When they were done, Willa leaned back on two hands and closed her eyes. "I may sink if we actually try to swim."

"A fine meal, but I'm not sure it holds a candle to your place."

She looked at him. "Thanks."

"Are you missing it?"

She took a moment to answer. "Actually, it's been nice to get away. The diner was my mama's place, and—"

"You've been filling her shoes?"

"In a way, I guess so." Willa stared at her empty glass.

"What did you study in college?"

She hesitated, and then, "Premed, believe it or not."

"Why wouldn't I believe it?"

A self-conscious shrug. "I didn't finish my last year. When Mama died I needed to be there for Katie."

"That's pretty admirable," he said.

"Not really. I've had my bouts of poor-me."

"Still admirable."

She met his gaze, disconcerted by the intensity in his eyes. "Haven't you done the same thing for Cline?"

"That's a little different," he said. "What happened to him shouldn't have happened. And if I hadn't—" He broke off there, shaking his head.

"So you do blame yourself," she said.

He was quiet for a few moments, his gaze set on the distant shoreline where a group of cows grazed. A white goose waddled along beside them.

"Sometimes it's hard not to," he said in a soft voice.

Sympathy squeezed at Willa's heart. She understood what it was to feel responsible for something that couldn't be changed. "My mom…she had a really hard time giving birth to Katie. She went through a lot of depression afterwards, and I don't think she ever really let herself bond with her. As Katie got older, it didn't get any better. And I don't know why exactly, but she never showed Katie any kind of…love. So I tried to give it to her. But kids are smart, and when Katie realized that Mama treated her differently from me, things changed between us."

"And Katie's directed her anger at you?"

"I guess she had to direct it at somebody."

"Doesn't really seem fair though, does it?"

"A lot of things aren't fair. They just are."

He studied her, blue eyes intense. "How'd you get so wise?"

"School of hard knocks." She shook her head then. "I guess I just realized at some point that all we can really do in this life is try to make it better from where we stand right now. We can't change what's already been done, no matter how much we want to do so."

He considered that and then said, "Sometimes I wish Cline would blame me."

"Would that really make anything better?" she asked.

He didn't answer, and they sat there for a while, the quiet strangely comfortable. A flock of geese flew over in a perfect V, their wings flapping in a rhythmic whoosh. A baby calf mooed for its mama, running across the field to find her.

"You want to talk about what happened this morning?" Owen asked, breaking the silence.

Willa said nothing for a moment, and then replied, "Two million dollars. I can hardly conceive of that much money."

"Don't you think you deserve it?"

"No. I guess I don't."

"Most people could find something to do with that kind of money."

"That's not the problem. My house has a laundry list of ailments. My car is on its last leg. The diner needs a face-lift, not to mention floors that are nearly worn through and a roof that leaks. But that doesn't mean I can accept it."

"He wanted you to have it."

"It doesn't seem right."

"To whom?"

"To Natalie. And did you see the look on his sisters' faces?"

"Priceless, wasn't it?"

"Owen, it's not funny."

"Sometimes people get caught with their greed

showing. I think Charles would have been amused by that."

"In their defense, I am something of a surprise."

"And it was your father who died. Your father who wanted to leave you something."

"It's kind of ironic," she said. "Right before you came to Pigeon Hollow, Judy asked me what I would do with the money if I won the lottery."

"And what did you say?"

"Silly stuff. The idea was too far-fetched to take seriously."

"But this is the real thing."

"I don't think I can let myself believe that."

"Sooner or later, you'll have to. For now, what do you say we go swimming?"

She brightened at the suggestion. "It's not too cold?"

He stood, offered her a hand and pulled her to her feet. "One way to find out. Come on."

She followed him to the side of the boat. He threw one leg over the rail, stood on the ledge, teetering.

"You're not really going to—" she began, just as he executed a perfect cannon ball into the water below.

He surfaced immediately, waving her in. "Chicken!"

That did it. She climbed over the rail, jumped,

and landing right beside him, came up sputtering a couple of seconds later. He wiped the water from his face. "Pretty good," he said.

"Pretty good?"

His smile was teasing, and they stared at one another, treading water. The sun warm on her back, Willa was suddenly, intensely, aware of something right and special passing between them. She started to say something, to break the moment.

But he put a finger on her lips and said, "Don't. Let's just let it be, okay?"

She looked into his eyes, saw the warm attraction there, felt its reflection somewhere inside her own heart. And let it be.

KATIE SPENT THE AFTERNOON helping Jake plant grass seed in a field being converted to pasture. She rode on the arm of his seat in the enclosed cab of the big green John Deere tractor. A week ago, she would have declared just the idea of riding around with somebody in overalls lamer than lame.

But there was something about being out here under a clear blue sky, bouncing along on the level ground, the smell of freshly turned dirt in the air, that made Katie glad Willa had forced her to come here. Not that she would admit as much to her sister.

She thought about Eddie, knew he wouldn't recognize her like this. Wondered then if it really mattered. Eddie was pretty much a loser. From this distance, even she could see that.

Jake stopped the tractor, letting the engine idle. He reached beneath his seat, pulled out two Mountain Dews and handed her one. He wasn't a big talker, but there was something about him that Katie found comforting. Like a grandpa was supposed to be. As if he'd been around a long time, had seen a lot of things, and not much got past him.

It was almost four o'clock when Jake headed the tractor back to the barn. "Feeding time," he said.

"Can I help?" she asked.

He pulled under a shed and cut the engine. "I've got a better idea. Cline usually goes swimming after school in the indoor pool. Why don't you go keep him company?"

"He swims?" Cloaked in astonishment, the question was out before she could edit it.

Jake smiled. "That boy's got more than a few surprises up his sleeve."

"I don't have a swimsuit," Katie said, doubting that Cline would want her there anyway.

"I believe there are some extras in the dressing room just off the pool. Go on now. You've been a good helper this afternoon. Time to have some fun."

She climbed down out of the cab, then looked back up at him. "Thanks, Jake."

He gave her a meaningful look. "And don't get any ideas about running off."

"I won't!" She jogged up the lane toward the house. The funny thing was, she didn't even want to.

CHAPTER TWELVE

WILLA AND OWEN SPENT the rest of the afternoon in the water, floating on the oversize rafts Owen pulled off the houseboat. It was a day Willa knew she would never forget. The cove so peaceful and quiet, they might have been the only two people on earth.

They talked. Staying away from serious stuff now. Just bits and pieces of each other's lives, forming a picture of who the other one was.

There were some major differences. He had gone to Columbia University; she had received a partial academic scholarship to the University of Louisville. He'd grown up surrounded by wealth and status. She had not.

But somehow, here in the quiet of this lake, none of it seemed to matter. What mattered was the connection between them, the sense that it wasn't something that came along every day.

"Can I ask you a personal question?" Owen turned his float so that they were face-to-face.

"Depends on how personal," she said, dragging her hand through the water and letting it slip through her fingers.

"Why isn't there anyone special in your life?"

She propped her chin on her forearms and looked him in the eye. "Who says there isn't?"

He tipped his head. "I figured if there was, you'd have mentioned him by now."

"Probably so."

When she didn't elaborate, he said, "Not answering, huh?"

"Not many guys my age are thrilled about built-in parenthood."

"Even so, I can't imagine you don't have to beat them off with a stick."

"That's pretty much exactly what's required for the men I meet in Pigeon Hollow."

"I can't blame them for trying." He was quiet for a moment, then said, "There was someone, wasn't there? Someone who hurt you."

She glanced up, then away, shook her head, even as the denial died on her lips. "I was engaged. To a guy I met in college. His name was Ashley. Ashley Morgan." The name sounded strange to her. She hadn't let herself say it out loud in so long.

"And?"

She drew in a deep breath, let it out again. "Oh,

you know. The worst kind of cliché. Wedding dress hanging in the closet. Invitations in the mail. Flowers at the church. And no groom."

"I can't begin to imagine what he was thinking."

His tone dismissed Ashley as an idiot. Which had its appeal. "I left school to take care of Katie. Turns out that didn't work for him. I guess I thought loving someone meant taking the difficult and making a go of it. I wanted it to be the real thing. But the truth?"

"What?"

"From the very beginning, I had this feeling. Deep inside. You know the kind that nags at you, but you ignore it because you don't want it to be true."

"Yeah," he said. "I know that feeling."

"So. Lesson learned? Gut instinct holds the winning hand every time."

"Maybe so, but like I said, the guy must have been an idiot."

"Thanks," she said.

"For what?"

"Trying to make me feel better."

"Added bonus. I wasn't trying to make you feel better. It's true."

She trailed her hand through the water, acknowledged her increasingly strong pull of attraction for him, even as she reminded herself this was exactly the kind of situation that had her gut instinct screaming Red Light.

"What are you thinking?" he asked, angling her float so she couldn't avoid his eyes.

"Honestly?"

"Honestly."

"That I like your smile," she said, sticking her toe over the line she had just drawn for herself. "It's the kind that makes other people want to smile."

He propped his chin on a fist, looking surprised by her answer. "I like yours, too."

She felt the flare between them, could not deny that she'd been the one to toss the match.

He moved her float again, this time bringing her up alongside him. They stayed that way for a few moments, just looking at one another, chins on folded arms, awareness a tangible current between them. The sudden return of common sense made her lower her eyes and say, "I don't think we should start down this path again."

"Probably not."

The lack of conviction in his voice rocked her own resolve. It had been a wonderful afternoon. The temptation to let it go where it would was strong. Dead-end roads, she reminded herself. She looked at him again and said, "We should be getting back, shouldn't we?"

"Yeah." Again she noted his reluctance.

A few yards away, a fish broke the surface of the water, making an enormous splash.

Owen nodded once, then pushed her float to the ladder. She slid off, and they climbed back on the boat, quiet. She went into the bathroom, dried off and changed into her clothes. When she came back out, he had changed as well. He put away the floats, pulled the anchor from the water.

Willa stood by the rail. The sun had started to sink, the air cooling considerably. The cows on the shore ambled across the pasture toward the barn visible in the distance, heading home.

She wished the day didn't have to end.

KATIE SPOTTED CLINE'S VAN at the side of the house next to a wheelchair ramp. A little bubble of compassion rose in her chest at the sight of it. How could a young guy like him accept that he would never walk again? She couldn't begin to even imagine not being able to run up the stairs, ride a bike, climb a tree. They were things she took for granted. Things he could no longer do.

The indoor pool sat to the left side of the house, connected by an open breezeway. Katie found the dressing room and the bathing suits Jake had told her would be there.

A pink bikini was the only one in her size. She

put it on and stood before the mirror, overcome with shyness at the thought of facing Cline in it.

Ridiculous. No guy had ever made her shy.

She headed for the pool door, opened it to a rush of warm air. It was like stepping into a tropical paradise. Square terra-cotta tile encased the perimeter of turquoise-blue water. Plump lounge chairs sat along the edges. In the lap lane, Cline swam toward the other end, muscled arms synchronized.

At the far end, he turned and swam back. When he reached the end of the pool, he surfaced at the side, pulling a pair of goggles over his head. Katie stood, suddenly uncertain of her welcome.

"Hey," she said.

"Hey."

"Jake said you might be here."

"Yeah." He propped his arms on the side of the pool and looked up at her, water glistening on the tips of thick lashes.

"I didn't know you…I mean—"

He tipped his head toward the wheelchair parked a few yards away. "Did you think I never got out of that thing?"

She lifted a shoulder, certain she was destined to be nothing more than a bumbling idiot around him.

He pressed his lips together. And then said,

"It's okay. I didn't know anything about paralyzed people either until I became one."

The remark felt like an admonition. "Maybe I should go," she said.

"You just got here."

"I know, but you'd probably rather be alone."

"No," he said. "I wouldn't. Stay."

THE HOUSEBOAT EASED out of the cove. Owen stood behind the wheel, his gaze on Willa's back where she lingered by the rail, looking out as if she were sorry they were leaving.

He wished they weren't. He wished he had kissed her, though he had no right to do so.

And wasn't that the point? He had no right.

He thought about his situation, how screwed up it was. He was beginning to realize that he had nothing to offer Pamela. And he was equally certain that given the direction he was headed in, Winding Creek Farm wouldn't be his much longer.

Unsettling as that was, Owen wondered at the timing of Willa's entrance in his life. Since the moment he'd set eyes on her, the very thought of marrying Pamela sat like a rock on his chest. And what had seemed reasonable now felt implausible.

He eased the throttle forward, the boat picking up speed. Just short of the bend leading out of the cove, it sputtered and came to a stop, silent. Waves washed back, tipping it left, right, left, right.

Willa crossed the boat and stood beside the wheel. "What's wrong?" she asked.

"I'm not sure," he said, turning the key and trying the engine. Completely dead. "Not good."

He checked the gas tank and oil. Glanced at the engine.

"Why don't you give it a few minutes?" she said.

They waited, and then he tried to crank it again. No go.

"I'd better call for help," he said. "It'll be dark soon."

He pulled his cell phone out of the glove compartment and switched it on. The no-service light blinked in bold orange. He groaned. "You're not going to believe this."

"Not working?"

He looked up at her. "I swear I didn't plan this."

"What do we do, swim for it?"

"An option, but we'd have a hike ahead of us. Let's hope Artis misses us at the marina. He knows I'm always back by dark."

Willa crossed the deck and sat down on a bench seat, the air cooling with the encroaching dusk. "So we wait."

Owen watched her for a moment, then walked

over and sat down beside her. Hands behind his head, he studied the darkening sky. "Most of the women I've dated would not have been happy at this turn of events."

"What do you mean?"

"Isn't it the female duty to be irritated when a guy messes up?"

She raised an eyebrow. "First of all, this wasn't anybody's fault. And second of all, maybe you haven't been dating the right women."

He caught her gaze, held it for a long moment. "Yeah," he said. "Maybe I haven't."

KATIE ROUNDED ONE side of the pool, walked down the steps and into the water. Cline tried not to stare.

He failed without question, unable to pull his gaze away from her impossible-not-to-notice curves.

She dove in, swam to the other side and then back. All the while, he watched her sure strokes, the neat precision with which she broke the surface of the water.

He turned away, put his goggles on, headed to the lane and continued with his laps. He completed six before finding the side of the pool again, dropping his head back to breathe in a few steady gulps of air.

"Nice." Katie bobbed in the water beside him.

"Thanks," he said.

"Did you swim—" She broke off there, leaving the question unfinished.

"Before?"

"Yeah."

"Not much. Running was my thing."

"That must have been hard to give up," she said in a soft voice.

"Not hard at all when you don't have a choice."

She bit her lip, and then whispered, "No matter what I say to you, it always feels like the wrong thing."

He thought about that—the fact that maybe he was being unfair to her. "That's me, not you," he said.

She blew out a sigh. "Maybe I really ought to go."

He should let her. They had little to nothing in common. What was the point in acting as if they ever would? Obvious as the answer was, he didn't want her to leave. "I'm sorry," he said.

She turned back from the steps, considering, and then swam over, floating on her back. "I used to go swimming at the Y in our town. Pretty nice that you have your own pool."

He leaned against the wall, resting his elbows on the sides to hold himself up. "I never used it much before."

"You're a good swimmer."

"Thanks."

"What else did you do before?"

The question again surprised him. Most people steered clear of anything hinting at *before*. She seemed determined not to ignore the elephant in the room. He liked her for it. "Rode dirt bikes, horses."

"You miss those things?"

"Yeah." He put his chin on his forearms, not looking at her. "Sometimes I dream about things I used to do. And there's a little window right before I wake up when I think my life is the way it used to be. That's the part that sucks the most. The moment I remember it isn't."

She rested her arms on the wall beside him. "I know a lot of guys who can walk and aren't anywhere near as together as you."

He looked at her, not sure what to say to that.

She grimaced. "That sounded stupid, didn't it?"

"No," he said. "It wasn't stupid. But I don't feel very together."

"Isn't that what being a teenager is all about?"

He gave her a half smile. Here in the water, it was as if they were equals. Like he was any normal guy talking to a cute girl. It was a feeling he didn't want to let go yet. "What do you do for kicks in Pigeon Hollow?"

She peered over at him through the most incredible eyes, thick-lashed and full of life. "Oh, there's the Friday night drag race out at Clark Thurman's place. Tobacco-spitting contest every third Saturday."

He laughed. "You don't look like the drag-racing type. Tobacco-spitting, either, come to think of it."

"I guess you think we're just a bunch of rednecks out there in the boonies," she said.

"Why would I think that?"

"That's what people usually think."

"I've never been one to go along with 'usually.'"

She gave him an appraising look. "No. I'd say you're not."

"I hear you have a boyfriend," he said, the words out before he had time to reconsider.

"Past tense," she said.

"What happened there?"

"Your brother kind of removed me from the situation."

"Willingly or unwillingly?"

"Unwillingly at the time."

"And now?"

She hesitated, then said, "I'm glad he did."

"So you changed your mind about this guy?"

She shrugged. "I guess I knew all along he wasn't the right thing."

"What was the draw?"

"Making Willa crazy."

Cline smiled. "What's the rift between you two?"

"There isn't one, really. She just thinks she needs to save me from myself."

"Does she?"

"I'm not sure that's possible."

He let that stand for a moment, then asked, "What's so bad about you?"

She didn't answer for a while. "That's what I've been trying to figure out my whole life."

"What makes you think there is something?"

She dropped her head back and stared up at the skylight above them. "A mom who wished I'd never been born for starters."

"That's a little harsh, isn't it?"

"If the truth is harsh, then I guess so."

The look on her face made him realize there was a well of pain behind her determined indifference. He wanted, suddenly, to make it better for her. Or at least to show her she wasn't the only one who felt like a disappointment. "I don't think my dad ever accepted that I'm going to be paralyzed for the rest of my life. Or maybe he just couldn't believe a son of his could be anything less than a full man."

Katie put a hand on his arm, the touch sending

a bolt of feeling straight through his chest. "Cline, you're a great-looking guy. Not to mention all the other things you've got going for you."

Something in her voice told him she wasn't just being nice. And that felt good. "My dad, he was pretty hard to figure. We barely learned the name of one girlfriend before he was on to another. Ironic considering this crazy provision he put in his will for Owen. He has to get engaged, or he's going to lose his inheritance."

"Wow. That sucks," Katie said.

"Having a say after you're gone. I guess that's not exactly like taking it with you, but close enough."

"Where's your mom?" she asked.

"South of France, last I heard. She wasn't exactly the maternal type, you know?"

"Yeah," she said. "I do."

Neither of them spoke for a while. And then Cline pushed off from the edge. "Race you to the other end?"

She plunged back into the water. "You're on."

CHAPTER THIRTEEN

HELP ARRIVED IN THE FORM of Artis just after nine o'clock that evening.

By that time, Willa's stomach was growling, but she didn't say anything because Owen already felt bad enough about the breakdown.

"Ahoy, there." Artis brought his bass fishing boat to a gliding stop just short of the pontoon. "Been lookin' all over for you two. Then I happened to remember this was your favorite spot."

"I was hoping you'd miss us," Owen said, reaching for the other man's rope. "We were beginning to think we'd have to swim for it."

"What's the problem?"

"Engine died. No service on the cell phone."

"Winning combination," Artis said, smiling. "Y'all hop on. Why don't you anchor her for the night? I'll come back and haul her in tomorrow morning, see if I can locate the problem."

They gathered their things and climbed on the boat. Artis sped off, pulling out his phone to call his wife and ask her to have a couple sandwiches ready for them.

Back at the marina, Owen thanked Artis for the rescue.

"Anytime," the older man said. "I'll let you know on the boat."

Madge came out with their sandwiches and twin cups of lemonade. "Bet you two are starving."

"This'll hit the spot," Owen said. "Thanks, Madge."

"Don't mention it."

They sat at a picnic table on the dock and made short work of their food without talking.

A young man in cutoff blue jean shorts and a white T-shirt walked by. He had a camera case on one shoulder, a duffel bag on the other.

He stopped a short distance away, turned around and looked at them, as if he were trying to figure out who they were. He pointed a finger at Owen and said, "Hey, aren't you—"

"Just leaving," Owen said, standing.

"Owen Miller. The guy with the inheritance problem."

"Look, it's late. We're—"

The man pulled out his camera, stepped back and aimed a shot at them. "Come on, be a sport. I'm with the *Daily Record*. We've been getting all kinds of letters asking whether you've taken the big leap."

"Don't take that picture," Owen said, his voice low with warning.

"One shot." The flash went off.

Owen reached for the camera, but the man backed up and sprinted off for the parking lot.

Willa stood up, stunned. "Why did he do that?"

Owen ran a hand through his hair, his face flushed. "Fodder for the gossip mill, no doubt."

"Because you're with me?"

"It doesn't matter," he said.

They walked out to his truck in silence. Once they were headed back down the road, he looked at her and said, "I'm sorry for being short. Guys like that just really get me going."

"You don't need to apologize."

He studied the road for a few moments, then glanced over at her. "I had a good time today, Willa."

"So did I," she said.

IT WAS AFTER MIDNIGHT when Willa tapped at Katie's door.

"Katie? It's me."

No answer. She quietly turned the knob and stepped into the room, Sam right behind her.

Katie faced the other way, asleep.

Willa walked around the bed, then sat down on the corner. With her barriers lowered this way, she reminded Willa of the little girl who had once looked up to her, cared what she thought. She smoothed a hand across her sister's hair, love for her welling up in a fierce wave.

"Oh, Katie, I know Mama did so many things wrong. If I could change any of those hurts, take them away for you, I would. I can't, but I love you. Shouldn't that count for something?"

Katie remained still. And Willa wondered why she had never said these things out loud to her before. But then the answer was clear. What if it didn't count? Where would they go from there?

AS SOON AS WILLA CLOSED the door behind her, Katie opened her eyes. She rolled over on her back, threw an arm above her head. A little knot of pain sat hard in her chest, the edges unfurling so that she felt singed, as if she'd leaned against a too-hot stove.

Love. Sometimes, she ached for it. Like she had a big hole inside her that could never be filled.

And yet she wouldn't let Willa in. Had shut her out and locked the door.

She rolled over and punched her pillow.

She *couldn't* let Willa in, because somewhere

deep down inside, Katie knew she wasn't lovable. If your own mother didn't love you, how could anyone else?

JUST AFTER ONE a.m., Owen gave up on trying to sleep, the hours he and Willa had spent together on the lake that afternoon replaying through his mind over and over again, each loop leaving him more convinced that he did not want it to end there.

He pulled on jeans and an old Columbia sweatshirt and let himself out of the house. The cool night air felt good on his face, a slight breeze lifting the leaves of the trees along the driveway. He walked fast, hands in his pockets, his head pounding with the need to come to terms with the truth that had taken root inside him.

He stopped short of the barn, leaned against the board fence, staring out at the moving shadows of the horses grazing in the pasture. He had grown up loving this farm. The thought of losing it turned like a knife in his heart.

He could marry Pamela and keep it all. But he didn't love her. And if he were honest with himself, he had known long before today, long before he met Willa Addison, that marriage between Pamela and him would be a mistake.

It had been his father's goal to force him to be

a more honorable man than he himself had been, to be the kind of man who committed to a relationship and stuck with it, the kind of man who did the right thing.

Ironically enough, for the first time in a long while, Owen thought he knew what that was.

WHEN WILLA AND SAM came downstairs the next morning, Natalie sat in the kitchen, drinking a cup of coffee.

"I'm sorry," Willa said. "I didn't realize you were—"

"Owen just left," she said. "I actually wanted to speak to you."

"Okay," Willa said.

Natalie gestured toward the coffeepot on the table. "I believe there's plenty if you'd like some."

"Thank you." Willa poured a cup and sat down on the opposite side of the table.

"You left so quickly yesterday, we didn't get a chance to talk."

"I know. I'm sorry." She took a sip of her coffee, and then said, "I can't accept that money."

She had thought about it last night in bed, long into the night.

"I have to say, that's the last thing I expected to hear," Natalie said, clearly surprised.

Willa looked down at her cup and then met the

woman's direct gaze. "I don't feel I have any right to it."

Natalie said nothing for a few moments, as if she needed time to figure out what to say. "I've never been one to pretend something is what it isn't. You were Charles's daughter, and I've accepted that. I admit, it wasn't so easy at first. But it was his wish that you be included in his will."

"It's so much money. That must take away from your—"

"My dear," she interrupted. "I loved my husband very much. He took good care of me. And he wanted to take care of you, too."

The sincerity in her voice tied a knot in Willa's heart, and she thought how gracious this woman was to put aside her own feelings in regard for her husband's.

"Would it help," Natalie said, "if there were a way you might get to know him better?"

Willa blinked, surprised. "How?"

"He kept journals over the years. Would you like to read them?"

Again, Willa didn't know what to say; Natalie's generosity was overwhelming. "Are you sure that's something you want to share?"

"I've given it a good bit of thought," she said. "I know it must be as hard for you to understand why Charles waited so long to see you as it has been for me to understand why he didn't tell me about you. Maybe this will help in some way."

OWEN HAD A nine o'clock meeting with a potential investor an hour's drive from Lexington. He called Pamela's house on the way, only to learn from her mother that she had gone to see her sister and would be returning the following day. He tried her cell phone and got her voice mail.

"Hey," he said. "We need to talk. Call me when you get back, and I'll drive out to your place."

He clicked off the phone, flipped the top closed. She deserved to hear this from him face-to-face. And the sooner they resolved it, the better.

NATALIE INVITED WILLA and Katie to stay at her home while Willa went through the journals. Willa thanked her, but told her they would find a place, not wanting to intrude on her privacy.

Natalie had just left when Katie walked into the kitchen and rubbed Sam under the chin. "Morning," she said.

"Good morning," Willa replied, startled by the lack of sullenness in her sister's voice.

Katie poured herself a glass of orange juice from the pitcher on the counter. "Was that Mrs. Hartmore leaving?"

"She came by to tell me that my father had kept journals. She's offered to let me read them."

Katie made a sound that wasn't approval or disapproval, something in between.

Willa started to tell her about the inheritance, but decided to wait until she was more certain of her own feelings. "What would you think about staying a few days longer?"

"Here?" Katie asked.

"Maybe it would be better if we found another place to stay."

Katie failed to hide a look of disappointment. "I kind of like helping out Jake."

Her response surprised Willa to say the least, untainted as it was by the belligerence she had grown so used to hearing in Katie's voice. Since they had been here, the change in Katie was noticeable. She and Cline had been spending more time together, and Willa wondered if it might have more to do with him than Jake. Whatever the impetus, the difference was gratifying. "I'll ask Owen."

Katie finished off her orange juice and made a more convincing display of nonchalance. "Whatever," she said. "I told Jake I'd help him do stalls this morning. I'll take Sam with me. Come on, Sam."

Katie darted out of the kitchen, and for the first

time in longer than she could remember, Willa felt hopeful that they might somehow find a way back.

LOUISA CAME IN SHORTLY AFTER Katie left, and Willa spent the morning helping her in the kitchen. Willa liked the other woman's quiet sense of humor. They shared some recipes, and at Louisa's request, she made her best-selling dessert from the diner.

"You're a wonderful cook," Louisa said when Willa pulled the meringue-covered coconut-cream pie from the oven. "That's perfect."

"My mother taught me how. At the time, I was pretty bored with it, but I'm glad for the skill now."

Louisa wiped her hands on her apron, and said, "Nothing like a woman's good cooking to keep a man in line."

"Is that all it takes?"

"It's a good part of the equation. Just as important as sex," she said with a wink and a nod.

"I'll file that one away," Willa said, smiling.

"You have a boyfriend at home?"

She shook her head. "No time for that right now."

Louisa clucked her disapproval. "Life's not what it should be if you don't make time for love. Or so I keep telling that Owen."

"He's had a lot of girlfriends?" As soon as the question was out, Willa wished she could take it back.

"Too many, if you ask me," Louisa said. "Just none of them the right one. That's the key. Finding the right one."

Louisa's words still echoed in Willa's thoughts later that afternoon when Owen arrived back at the house. He walked into the living room where she had been trying, unsuccessfully, to read, her thoughts everywhere except on the page in front of her.

He wore a light gray suit with a white shirt and red tie, which he loosened at his throat. "Sorry to desert you today," he said.

"Don't be." She hesitated, and then said, "About yesterday—"

"If you're going to say none of it should have happened, please don't. I look at you, Willa, and for the first time I can remember, it feels like maybe I'm looking at something that could be really, really right."

The words fell over her, sincere, imploring. "Wrong time," she said softly. "Natalie offered to let me read the journals Charles left. I think it would be best if Katie and I found another place to stay."

"There's no reason why you can't stay here," Owen said.

"Yeah. There is." She stood then, and placing the book on the coffee table, left the room.

OWEN WAITED A WHILE and then walked down to the barn, hoping Willa had headed that way.

She stood by the riding ring, watching Katie trot around on one of the older mares they used in the summer children's camp. Sam lay on the grass beside her, panting.

"Hey," he said.

She turned her head to look at him. "Hey."

"She looks good out there."

"She does. I haven't seen Katie take interest in anything other than being rebellious in so long. I'm grateful to you for letting us come here. It's been really good for her."

He considered the words, and then said, "Pamela is out of town. I'm going to talk to her tomorrow when she gets back. We have some loose ends to settle. But there's no reason for you and Katie to go somewhere else, Willa. We should be able to deal with this like adults."

She looked at him for a long moment, then glanced out at Katie, and said, "Okay. And again, thank you. For everything."

Owen nodded once, put his elbows on the top board of the fence, only then admitting he had been holding his breath for her answer.

THAT EVENING, WILLA called Judy. She tried her at home first, and when there was no answer, dialed the diner number, even though it was after nine o'clock.

Judy answered, sounding tired.

"You're still there?" Willa asked.

"Hey you," Judy said, her voice brightening too quickly. "Yeah, it beats going home, you know?"

Willa did know. Knew what it was like to prefer peace, however it might be found. "Judy—"

"Don't, okay? I've been the one wearing the dunce cap, but I think I've finally come to my senses. There are far worse things than being alone."

"Oh, Judy—"

"No sympathy, okay? This is something I've needed to do for a long time. So tell me what's going on," she said, clearly changing the subject.

Willa brought her up to date, told her about Charles and the inheritance, as well as her misgivings about it.

"And you're considering not taking it?" Judy blurted in disbelief. "No, but of course, you're thinking about it. Willa! When are you ever going to believe that you have a right to something good coming along in your life?"

"Maybe on the day you believe the same about yourself."

Judy sighed. "Honey, you better think about this long and hard. This diner's a fine business, but we both know you're stretched thin by the end of the month."

"Should that be a reason to accept it?"

"Do you need a reason? The man obviously wanted you to have it."

"I don't know, Judy. It's all been really strange. He left some journals. His wife has offered to let me read them. I'd like to stay a while longer and do that if you can—"

"Of course, I can."

"Thanks, Judy. You're the best."

"Go on now," she said, a smile in her voice.

They talked of other things then, Willa telling her about the changes in Katie.

"That child is enough like you that she's bound to turn out all right," Judy said. "You planning on filling me in on that hunky Owen?"

Willa stalled, recalling Owen's words from earlier. Loose ends to settle. She wished she'd had the courage to ask him what he'd meant by that. "I'm not exactly sure what's going on, she said, "It's a little complicated."

"Ah, but you see, anything worth having usually is."

CHAPTER FOURTEEN

THE NEXT MORNING, Natalie drove over with several boxes containing the leather-bound journals. Owen had again already left the house when Willa came downstairs. He'd left a note offering the use of an extra office on the main floor where she could read.

Once Natalie had driven away, Willa went into the room, waited for Sam to trot in behind her, then closed the door. She sat down in the chair behind the desk. The journals had been organized in chronological order. She picked up the first, studied the cover for a few moments, uncertain about opening it.

The label on front read: July–September 1958.

Charles would have been around twenty years old. A young man with life ahead of him.

Her hand shook a little as she turned to the first page. The handwriting was neat, the blue ink slightly faded against the white paper.

School today. Dad still up in the air about the biochem class I'm taking. Just the thought that I might actually buck the system and choose med school over following in his footsteps has him in a pretzel of worry.

A small shiver skittered down Willa's back. Charles had wanted to be a doctor? She rubbed her arms, staring again at the words. Since her first toy medical kit, that had been her life goal.

She thought about her own dream, of how she'd let it go. Let herself fall into a life that wasn't of her design.

What had happened to make her father choose another direction?

She turned the page and read on.

IT WAS ALMOST SEVEN O'CLOCK when Owen arrived home that evening. He'd been in meetings all afternoon with several breeders concerned about the recent interest of a group of investors in some of Lexington's biggest farms.

Pamela's car sat in the driveway. He propped an elbow on the doorsill, pressed two fingers to his left temple, willing the pounding to stop. The headache had nagged at him throughout the day, and now picked up its tempo.

He left the vehicle outside the garage, got out

and went inside the house. Voices carried from the living room.

He stopped in the doorway. Willa stood behind a leather chair, her fingers clasped at the top of the cushion. Pamela sat on the couch, legs crossed, a newspaper on her lap.

"Owen," she said. "Your message sounded as if it were important so I came straight here."

"I'll be upstairs," Willa said.

"Don't go yet," Pamela said, holding up a hand. "I was just about to congratulate you for making local headlines."

She handed the paper to Owen. He unfolded it. The photo from the night at the marina took up the center of the page. He frowned, folding it back up.

"Have you enjoyed making a fool of me, Owen?" Pamela's voice rose on a shrill note.

"It wasn't like that," he said softly.

"Then what was it?" She set her gaze on Willa. "I've been trying to figure out what you're thinking, Owen. No offense, but would I be too far off base to say she's not your normal type?"

"Pamela," Owen warned.

"So what is it? Are you thinking this little heiress from Hicksville can get you out of your bind?"

"That's enough," he said, steel in his voice.

Willa started to say something, pressed her lips together, then walked out.

"Willa, wait," Owen said, but she kept going, closing the door behind her.

Pamela dropped onto the couch, crossed her legs and pulled a pack of cigarettes out of her purse. She lit one and inhaled deeply. She released a stream of smoke, and said, "What would you have me do, Owen? We've been going out for a year. Was I wrong to expect something to come from that?"

"No," he said, his anger at her smothered by a sudden cloud of regret. "You weren't. But you had no right to say those things to Willa. She's done nothing wrong."

"Not for lack of coercion?"

"Pamela." He ran a hand through his hair, sighed deeply. "I didn't plan any of this. I didn't go looking for it."

"Damn you, Owen," she said, stubbing the cigarette out in a nearby ashtray. "Was I nothing more than an answer to your inheritance problem, or just the stand-in until something more appealing came along?"

"It wasn't like that," he said. "I never meant to hurt you. You deserve better than the way I've handled this."

She folded her arms across her chest. "You're right. I do."

"I'm sorry," he said.

"And that makes it all better?"

"No. It's just the truth," he said quietly.

She stood, hung her purse on her shoulder. "I guess that's clear enough for me."

She walked out of the room then, the front door clicking closed behind her a few seconds later.

From the living room window, Owen watched her get into her car, remorse stabbing at him. Not for the end of their relationship. Right or wrong, he felt relief in that. But for not admitting sooner what a mistake they would have made in staying together for any other reason than the only one that mattered. Love.

FRESH FROM THE SHOWER, Katie dried her hair and shrugged into a pair of blue jeans and a slim-fitting white T-shirt. She slipped on a pair of sandals, and headed downstairs, hoping to run into Cline.

That afternoon, she'd gone with Jake to pick up a mare and foal from a local veterinary hospital where they had been for the past week after complications during the delivery.

Katie had been fascinated by the place, taking in the sights and sounds, the words of the veterinarian explaining the mare's case to Jake.

When she'd been a little girl, Katie had dreamed of becoming a vet. She loved animals and couldn't imagine a better way to make a living than by taking care of them. But that was before she'd decided to major in flunking out of school. Such options were now long lost to her.

She found Cline at his computer, a couple of hefty textbooks open on the desk.

She stopped in the doorway, suddenly unsure of interrupting. "Hey," she said.

He looked up, smiled as if he were glad to see her.

She smiled back.

"Where you been?" he asked. "Thought you might come out for a swim this afternoon."

"I went with Jake to the vet hospital."

He leaned back in his chair. "Bore you to death?"

"No. Actually, I loved it."

He raised an eyebrow. "Hidden aspirations?"

She bit her lip, shrugged, not a yes, not a no.

"A vet, huh?"

She shook her head. "I don't have the grades."

"A little early to throw in the towel, isn't it?"

"At school, I'm what's known as a lost cause."

He gave that some consideration, biting his lower lip. "Come here," he said.

She walked over to the desk, cautious. "What?"

He moved the mouse to his computer, tapped on the keyboard for a few moments, and then pointed at the monitor. "See that?"

She looked at the screen, read out loud. "Genetic Engineering and the Intrinsic Value and Integrity of Animals and Plants. Wow. Is this the kind of stuff you've been looking at?"

"It's what I want to do when I grow up," he said, a smile in his voice.

"Aren't there all sorts of ethical questions to consider in a field like that?"

"That's one of the things that makes it fascinating. It seems really important that people with the right motivations get into it."

"Cool," she said, impressed.

"I think so."

"It must be a good feeling, to set your sights on something in the future and want to be a part of it."

"I didn't say I was going to make it. Who knows? But I'm going to give it my best shot."

"You'll make it," she said.

"No reason you can't do the same," he said softly.

She shoved her hands in her pockets. "Sometimes, it's just too late."

"Jeez," he said. "Sixteen, and you're writing off life. Look at this."

He typed in a phrase in the search engine, hit enter and sat back. A few seconds later, a home page booted up. Virginia-Maryland Regional College of Veterinary Medicine. He clicked on Admissions. Then Admission Requirements. "That could be you," he said. "And that's just one school. Happens to be a good one. You could go there."

She began to shake her head. "I couldn't—"

"Why not?" he interrupted. "Katie, I'm not much older than you. When I first became paralyzed, I pretty much decided I was going to spend the rest of my life being bitter. Wishing for what was, what could never be again. That got old fast. I decided I needed to find something else to put all that energy into."

She didn't say anything for a moment. "And you chose the future."

"So can you," he said, his eyes shining with certainty.

For the first time in her life, Katie believed it might just be true.

KATIE CAME UPSTAIRS around ten-thirty, and Willa went over to say good-night. Her sister's response was distracted, but without its normal edge. When Willa asked what she'd been doing, she said, "Hanging out with Cline."

She left it at that and went back to her room where Sam lay on the rug, snoring softly. She sat on the bed and tried not to think about what had happened downstairs with Pamela, about the fact that she and Owen might be making up at that very moment.

She reached for the journal she had left on the nightstand earlier, sat back against the pillows and began reading.

For the next couple of hours, she absorbed herself in the words on the page, discovering that her father had indeed given in to pressure from his family and decided against medical school.

At certain points, his regret was palpable, and Willa felt its echo within herself.

The entries were sporadic, sections of time where he wrote something nearly every day, and then others where entire months were skipped. It was an odd feeling to witness the unfolding of a person's life, her father's life, the ordinary with the extraordinary.

The sight of her mother's name against a yellowing page sent a start of adrenaline through her veins, and she realized she had been waiting to reach this point with a mix of anticipation and trepidation.

The entry was marked: Tanya, August 1, 1977.

She drank in the words without being aware of breathing. The night they met. The quick attraction that flared between them. The postponing of his trip home, and the ensuing two days they had spent together.

She read on, transfixed by the chance meeting that had led to her very existence. In the pages that followed were evidence of Charles's regret, and it was double-fold for the pain he had caused Willa's mother, and the pain he had caused Natalie, his fiancée.

Not wanting to read anymore, Willa closed the journal, sat with her hand on its leather cover, wondering if this had been the turning point for her mom, if bitterness had seeped into every relationship that had followed the disappointment of this one.

A knock sounded at the door. She put the journal on the nightstand and said, "Come in."

Owen stepped into the room. He looked tired. "Hi."

"Hi," she said, her heart picking up tempo at the sight of him.

Sam opened his eyes, wagged his tail, then went back to sleep.

"Can we talk?" Owen asked.

"I—sure." She slid off the bed and stood, straightening her clothes.

He tipped his head at the journal lying beside the lamp. "How's it going?"

She lifted her hands. "It's a little unsettling,

seeing what happened back then, but now I understand my mother's disillusion a bit better."

"I guess people don't always meet at the right time in their lives."

"No. But they still have to think about who they might hurt."

The parallel to what was happening between the two of them hung like a tangible presence in the room. They said nothing for a few moments, and then Owen spoke. "What happened downstairs. I'm sorry."

"It's okay."

He nodded once. "Well, I better let you get some sleep."

"Yeah. It's late."

He walked to the door. Hand on the knob, he turned back. "It's over between Pamela and me."

Willa glanced away and then met his gaze. "Are you all right with that?"

He didn't answer for a moment, and then said, "I should have ended it a long time ago. When something's not right, it's not right. I owed it to her to be honest about that."

"Fair enough," she said quietly.

He let himself out of the room, the door clicking closed behind him.

She didn't move until she could no longer hear his footsteps in the hall.

NATALIE CALLED on Friday morning.

Louisa handed Willa the phone in the kitchen where she stood pouring a cup of coffee.

"Sorry to be calling so early," Natalie said. "But I've thrown together a small dinner party tonight for some of Charles's friends. I'm hoping you can come."

The invitation caught Willa off guard. "Oh. Well. That sounds nice."

"Wonderful. Bring Owen. And Cline and your sister, too."

"Okay," Willa said, unsure about going, but equally certain she couldn't say no.

"I'll see you then," Natalie said.

Owen called later that day from an auction where he planned to bid on a very desirable mare he had been hoping to purchase for some time. When Willa told him about the dinner, he said he would meet them there.

That evening Cline offered to drive them in his customized van. Katie sat up front, wearing a light blue sleeveless dress that looked great on her. Willa, in the back seat, looked down at her own peach linen skirt and top, hoping it would be appropriate.

The house was lit up, a dozen or so cars lining the cobblestone courtyard. Cline parked, and they all went in, Willa's stomach tipsy with nerves.

Natalie greeted them at the doorway, kissed Cline on the cheek, then took Willa's arm and looped the other through Katie's. She led them to the edge of the living room. "Excuse me, everyone," she said.

The crowd grew quiet, all eyes focused on them. "I would like to introduce Willa Addison, Charles's daughter. And this pretty young girl is her sister, Katie. I hope you will all make them feel welcome this evening."

People nodded in their direction, offered curious smiles.

Willa talked with Natalie for a while about the journals, the older woman appearing to enjoy hearing some of the things she had learned about Charles. The year-long excursion he had made across Europe in his twenties with nothing but a backpack and a rail pass. The time he had decided to grow his own garden and planted so much squash, he'd had to give bushels of it away.

Natalie's smile was wistful. "Hearing you talk about him brings a little piece of him back."

Owen arrived just as everyone sat down for dinner. "I'm sorry for being so late," he said, kissing Natalie on the cheek.

"Don't be," she said, indicating the empty chair next to Willa. "We saved you a place."

Willa glanced up at him, her smile faltering. He looked devastating in a dark suit and light blue shirt. His tie, a bright green with flecks of navy, managed to take the seriousness out of the look.

"Hey," he said, ducking his head close to hers.

She toyed with the stem of her wineglass, dropping her gaze. "Hey."

"The trick is," he said, sitting down beside her, "to picture them all doing something that makes them just as human as the rest of us."

Willa smiled. "I'm afraid to ask for suggestions."

He tipped his head at the other end of the table, where Cline and Katie were engrossed in what looked like a debate of some sort. "Those two doing all right?"

"Seems so. They were actually talking about colleges on the way over here. I've never heard Katie mention the word."

Owen looked impressed. "Maybe she's turned a corner."

"I don't know, but if so, Cline's had a lot to do with it."

"I suspect Katie's been good for him as well."

Dessert and coffee were served in the living room. Willa poured herself a cup while Owen chatted with one of Charles's former business partners.

Natalie touched a hand to her arm and said, "Was it as bad as you thought?"

"No." Willa smiled. "Thank you for this. It's beyond generous."

"But my dear, selfish, too. In you, part of Charles still lives."

CHAPTER FIFTEEN

OWEN ASKED IF Willa would like to ride back with him, freeing Cline and Katie to leave a little earlier.

They drove most of the way in silence.

In the driveway of his house, Owen turned off the engine to the Rover, dropped the keys on the dashboard. "Are you all right?"

"A little tired, I guess," she said.

"Feel like a walk?"

"I should go on in—" she began.

"A short one?"

"Okay. A short one."

They headed toward the barn, the moon lighting the way like an enormous lamp. Owen opened the big sliding center doors, and they stepped inside. A horse halfway down the aisle whinnied in greeting.

Owen opened a smaller door to one side of the main entrance, flicked on the light. Saddle racks lined one entire wall of the room, bridles hanging on an adjacent wall. It smelled of leather. A sofa sat in the middle of the floor, a coffee table in front of it. In the far corner was an old drink cooler, the kind with the slide-top lid.

"Coke?" Owen offered.

"Sure."

He crossed the pinewood floor and pulled out two glass bottles, popped the tops on the opener hanging from the wall and handed one to her.

She took a sip, wiped a finger at the corner of her mouth. "They just taste better in bottles, don't they?"

He smiled. "I always thought so."

Willa found herself caught up in that smile, wondered how he managed to use it so effectively. But then that wasn't really fair because there was nothing fake about Owen's charm.

"You were a hit tonight," he said.

"Everyone was very kind."

He sat down on the sofa and waved a hand for her to join him. She rested an arm against the back, angled a knee in his direction.

"You said that as if you deserve something less," he said softly.

"Did I?"

He held her gaze, warm interest flickering in his eyes. "I know I've said it before, but Willa, you have a right to everything you're getting from Charles."

She rubbed a finger across the condensation building on the Coke bottle. "That's the part I'm having trouble with. How a girl like me can go from famine to feast in the span of a few weeks."

"Life can change fast. Not always for the better."

She heard the sudden note of disquiet in his voice, knew he was thinking of Cline. "I'm sorry. I must sound petty."

"No. Actually, you're pretty amazing."

"Cowards aren't amazing."

He blinked wide. "What makes you a coward?"

She looked down at her lap. "Giving up."

"On what?"

"Things I wanted." She was silent for a moment and then said, "I wanted to be a doctor. Did you know that's what Charles wanted to be?"

"He told me once. Said he regretted not following through with it."

"That's kind of sad, don't you think?"

"Yeah. I guess it is. But who says it's too late for you, Willa?"

She shook her head. "Sometimes, it just is."

"It doesn't have to be."

"My mama always said the higher you reach, the farther the fall. That's kind of how she lived her life, I guess. Not reaching."

"Is that how you want to live yours?"

She wanted to say no, but wasn't that exactly what she had done?

They looked at each other for a few moments, a new intensity charging the air between them.

She should look away. Break the moment. She should. But she didn't.

He ducked in then, fast, as if not wanting to give either of them a chance to change their minds.

The kiss was sweet, unrestrained. Willa closed her eyes and kissed him back, closing off thoughts of anything but the rush of pleasure heating her blood.

They kissed for a good long while, the kind of kisses that clouded what had previously been clear thinking. Made nonsense of any argument impertinent enough to raise a cautionary red flag.

He smoothed a thumb across her bottom lip, the action rawly sensual. "Here we go again," he said.

"Um," she said, eyes closed.

"Should I apologize?" His mouth now found her ear, the words barely audible.

"Ah, no," she murmured with irony.

"All right if we try it again then?"

She didn't answer, but this time, leaned in and kissed him.

With a hand at the back of her neck, he deepened the kiss, the only sounds in the room the quickening of their breaths, the rustle of clothing against the leather couch, the scent of hay drifting through from the barn.

He took her Coke, set it on the coffee table. They changed leads, and he leaned into her, settling her against a pile of pillows, then stretching out alongside her, one hand firm along the outside of her thigh.

She dropped her head to one side.

With the back of his fingers he brushed her hair away, kissed her neck. Ah. Hot summer day. First plunge off the dock into cool lake water. Erupting back to the surface, exhilarated. Kissing Owen was like that. The best sensations she had ever known rolled into a single moment.

His mouth found hers again. His hands, purposeful, knowing, explored the length of her arms, the back of her knee, the curve of her calf. He said words she could have listened to for the rest of her life, words every woman wants to hear said of herself, never quite imagining they would actually come from a man like him.

He touched her as if he wanted to know all of her, as if she were something he might have once hoped for, but never really believed he would find.

She ran her own hands across the width of his shoulders, down the carved muscles of his arms, settled on his strong back.

Being with Owen made her realize how much

she had missed having a man in her life, missed this, touching and being touched, wanting and being wanted. And yet, even as the thought crossed her mind, she corrected herself. Not just any man. But this man. How easy it would be to lose herself in him.

A truck rolled by outside the barn, breaking the silence. Willa sat up suddenly, smoothed her hands across her skirt.

"That's Jake," Owen said, the words rough at the edges. "He must have gone out somewhere tonight."

Willa ran a hand through her hair and planted an elbow on her knee. "I should get back," she said, her voice not sounding like her own.

He straightened. "Are you okay?"

"Yes. But I should go," she whispered softly, then stood abruptly, tucking her hair behind her ears.

"Willa—"

She moved to the door, not trusting herself to answer.

He put their Coke bottles away, then flicked off the light.

They left the barn and walked without speaking back to the house. Owen opened the front door, and they stepped inside the foyer.

He leaned against the side of an enormous old

grandfather clock, arms folded across his chest. "Wanna tell me what happened just now?"

She stood at the foot of the staircase. "Have you ever had the feeling that maybe something is just too good to be true? This whole thing, my father, you—"

"I'm an optimist," he said. "I believe in good."

He walked over to the stairs then, standing close, his face inches from hers. He kissed her again, and there was promise at its edges, fragile, but there all the same.

CLINE ROLLED INTO THE FOYER the moment Willa went upstairs.

He raised an eyebrow, looked impressed. "So that's what happened to Pamela?"

Owen headed for the living room. "It's not like that."

"Like what then?" Cline asked, following.

Owen sat down in a chair next to the fireplace, dropped his head back against the cushion, palms behind his neck. "Of all the times in my life I could have met a woman like her, why now?"

"Why not now? You need a wife. All the better if you happen to be hot for her."

Owen gave his brother a look. "Not quite that simple."

"It should be."

"Oh, yeah, we've known each other a little more than a week, and I'm going to ask her to marry me."

"People who've known each other twenty-four hours fly to Vegas and get married by Elvis. Weirder things have happened."

Owen looked his brother in the eye. "It's not a big deal if the farm goes to you."

Cline held up both hands. "Whoa. You love this place. And I'm not planning on being here to run it."

Owen sighed and ran a palm over his face.

"It's your life in the balance," Cline said. "I don't blame you for not wanting to marry someone you aren't in love with. But, Willa? She's not like Pamela."

"I know," Owen said. Willa? She wasn't like anyone he'd ever known.

WILLA TOOK A STACK of journals down to the office on Saturday morning, planning to spend the day there.

It was hard to concentrate though when she couldn't stop thinking about last night. About kissing Owen.

That she was attracted to him, she could not deny. The kind of attraction that fogged the mirror of common sense until the shape of reason was too distorted to recognize.

And last night on that couch with Owen, she had very nearly let herself ignore the caution lights blaring all around her. The main one, of course, being Owen's inheritance problem.

Pamela's voice echoed now in her thoughts. *Are you thinking this little heiress from Hicksville can get you out of your bind?*

Maybe Pamela had asked the question out of sheer vindictiveness, but then again, Willa had her own questions about whether Owen would ever have noticed a woman like her had he not been doing a friend a favor.

She had her own history to blame for her self-doubts. But disappointment of the magnitude she had known did not create the desire for a repeat performance.

And so, she had pulled back last night and put some walls in place. Even though leaving had been the last thing she'd wanted.

Just after noon, a light knock sounded at the door.

"Come in," Willa said.

Natalie stepped into the room, her blond hair loose today. She carried a small box.

Sam went to greet her, nails clicking on the hardwood floor.

Natalie rubbed his ear, then looked at Willa. "I found a few more journals," she said. "I was cleaning out Charles's desk this morning. I'm not sure where they fit into what you've already read, but I thought you might want them."

"Thank you," Willa said, crossing the floor to take the box from her. "And thank you again for last night, Natalie. It was incredibly generous of you."

"You're more than welcome. But it wasn't really. I'm trying to learn from my husband's mistakes. I know now that he spent so many years wishing he had known you. I also know it caused him a great deal of pain. I think in the end, it's the things we don't do that leave us with the most regret."

Willa pressed her hands together, considered the truth behind the words. To date, it had certainly been accurate in her own life.

"You and Owen," Natalie said. "Is there something between you?"

A few seconds passed before she said, "Friendship, I hope."

"Ah." Natalie smiled. "Maybe my intuition is getting a little rusty in its old age, but I would have guessed at more."

"Owen is—"

"A terrific young man," Natalie inserted.

"In a complicated situation," Willa finished.

"Granted. But I think your father would tell

you that opportunities don't often come around a second time."

For a long time after Natalie left, Willa thought about that and the fact that last night she had chosen to see Owen as a risk. But sometimes, depending on the angle, maybe that was the same thing as a possibility.

KATIE LET HERSELF out the back door of the house and headed for the barn. The sun was already warm on her shoulders, and she looked forward to the day ahead.

It was like that here. She woke up excited to see what would happen next.

Jake had promised to let her give one of the horses a bath today. He'd already taught her how to pull a mane, trim whiskers and ears, comb out a tail without damaging it.

She wondered how she could be the same person she'd been in Pigeon Hollow. When she thought about all the energy she had put into being bad, shame heated her skin.

"Hey, Katie!"

She swung around. Cline waved from the raised window of his bedroom.

"Hey, there's a party tonight. Parents off premises."

"Yeah?"

"Wanna go?"

Katie smiled. "I should check my calendar first."

He smiled back. "If it's clear, we'll leave at six."

"Okay," she said.

The window slid closed, and he was gone.

Katie stood for a moment, enjoying the warm sun on her face. She took off at a run for the barn then, still smiling.

MIDAFTERNOON, a white envelope appeared beneath the office door.

Willa opened it, pulling out a single card.

Will you please have dinner with me tonight? If so, we'll leave at five o'clock. Check your answer below.
Yes
No
Return under door.

She reread the note. Ran a finger across the words.

A risk.

Or a possibility.

She'd lived most of her adult life in the center of the trampoline, refusing to get anywhere near the edges. She knew what it felt like to bounce too high and end up on the ground.

But some part of her had grown tired of always playing it safe.

So here it was. She could be a chicken for the rest of her life. Or test those boundaries.

She went back to the desk for a pen. And checked Yes. Yes.

CHAPTER SIXTEEN

A NOTE TAPED to her bedroom door read: *Wear something casual.*

Intrigued, Willa dressed in jeans and a light blue sleeveless blouse. It was simple with a fitted cut, and Judy had once said the color did nice things for her eyes.

She took some extra time blow-drying her hair with a big roller brush, leaving it loose at her shoulders. She slid her feet into chunky black sandals, then applied a light pink lipstick to her lips.

Sam sat just outside the bathroom door, watching her. She turned, waved a hand at her efforts. "Too much?"

His ears perked up in acknowledgment of the question. He lay down then and closed his eyes.

"You're no help," she said. "Are you pouting because I said you couldn't come along?"

He cracked an eye at her.

"And don't try to pretend Louisa's not giving

you cookies every time you give her one of those looks. I know better."

"Willa?"

She stuck her head out of the bathroom, found Katie standing just inside the bedroom door. "Hey. I didn't hear you come in."

"Wow. You look great," Katie said.

Willa brushed a self-conscious hand across her jeans. "Thanks."

"Where are you going?"

"Just dinner with Owen. No big deal."

"No big deal. I think it's great," Katie said, looking pleased.

Willa started to downplay the evening again, but stopped herself. "Actually, I'm looking forward to it."

"It's about time you had a real date."

"I don't know if this—"

"It will be if you let it."

"Hey, who's the big sister here?" Willa teased.

Katie smiled, and in that moment, it was the way it used to be between them. Sisters. Just that.

"Cline invited me to a party tonight," Katie said. "All right if I go?"

Willa's gaze widened. Had Katie really just asked her permission? "Sure. I don't see why not."

"Cool." She turned for the door, then swung back. "Hey, Willa?"

"Yeah?"

"Have fun, okay?"

Willa raised a hand, swallowing hard. "You, too."

OWEN STOOD IN THE FOYER, the smile on his face the kind of smile that could, without question, lead to big, big trouble.

Willa stopped at the foot of the stairs, acknowledged her own susceptibility to it. "Are you going to tell me what we're doing?"

"You like surprises?"

"I do," she said.

"Good. Then I'd like to surprise you."

They walked past the Range Rover in the driveway and headed to the barn where he packed their stuff up in the back of an old green Dodge pickup. Owen came around and opened her door.

The second surprise came when he drove away from the main road, toward one of the pastures behind the barn. He opened the gate, pulled through, then got out to shut it before driving on.

They drove for a half mile, went through another gate, and then hit a narrow dirt road that wound through a wooded area, before beginning an ascent up a fairly steep mountain.

Owen glanced at her. "We call her the Old Goat."

"The truck or the eating establishment you're taking me to?"

He laughed. "The truck."

"Should I be worried?"

"She's reliable."

Willa glanced out her window at the drop-off just over the shoulder. She inched away from the door. "And by now I'm guessing there's no restaurant at the top of this mountain."

He grinned. "I promised you dinner. I intend to keep my word."

They drove for another twenty minutes, the old truck's engine growling its way up the steep incline. The drive was beautiful, winding through hardwood trees that dappled the road with evening shade. At the top, the road leveled out, wound on for another quarter mile or so, then came to an abrupt end.

In front of them stood a weathered log cabin, the late afternoon sun glinting off its metal roof. A porch ran the width of the structure, wooden swings hanging on each end. To the left of the cabin lay the most beautiful pond she had ever seen. A group of white, orange-bill ducks glided across its center. At the edge of the cabin yard, a dock jutted out into the water.

Owen pulled the truck to the end of the dirt road. *"Maison de Bonne Cuisine."*

"Are we the first to arrive?" she asked, her tone teasing.

"We've booked the place for the evening."

"Um," she said. "You're in tight with the maître d'?"

He smiled a knee-weakening smile. "You could say that."

"You're determined not to stick with my original appraisal of you."

"Oh, yeah, squash-playing, cigar-smoking, man about town?"

She winced. "Sorry."

Owen laughed. "I'm pleased beyond words to have disappointed you."

He got out then, came around and opened her door. She slid to the ground, bumping up against him. He righted her with a steady hand, and they held each other's gaze for a moment, something electric popping between them.

He reached in the truck's bed, pulled out a picnic basket and a thick hand-sewn quilt, then waved her toward the front porch. The door was unlocked, and they stepped inside to a large open area. The kitchen sat on the right, dated refrigerator and stove positioned side by side. A living area held a couch and two chairs arranged around a dry-stack rock fireplace.

A lamp burned on an end table. "I came up earlier to check things out," Owen said. "No one's been here in a while."

"When it's not doubling as a restaurant, what do you use it for?"

He put the basket on the table, dropped the quilt onto a ladder-back chair. "I used to bring Cline up for campouts. We'd fish and hike. He loved coming up here." A shadow crossed his face. "I don't think he'd want to come anymore."

"Have you asked him?" Willa's voice was soft with sympathy.

Owen shook his head. "I've wanted to, but—"

Willa heard the defeat in his voice, wished for a way to erase the pain behind it.

"Okay," he said, "let's get this evening started. Ladies' room right through there. Meet you outside by the dock?"

She nodded and headed for the narrow hall he'd directed her to.

A few minutes later, she stepped outside, the sun already starting to set.

Owen stood on the dock, an old-fashioned wooden rowboat tied to the side.

"Your chariot awaits," he said.

"When you aim to surprise, you don't miss the mark."

He held her hand while she stepped down into the boat, his grip warm and firm. She took a seat on one end, Owen took the other. He picked up a set of oars and started rowing, the motions sure and strong, as if it were something he had learned long ago.

Willa's eyes went to the contours of his shoulders, the give and take of muscles used to challenge. She forced her gaze elsewhere.

A pair of deer stood at the water's edge, taking an evening drink. Spotting them, they darted away. "It's beautiful here," she said.

Owen stopped the boat in the center of the pond, reached behind him and pulled out a bottle of white wine. From a plastic cooler, he removed two glasses, the sides frosty cold.

"I think you were right," she said. "This has to be the best place in town."

He smiled, popped the cork and poured her a glass. He poured one for himself, then tapped the rim against hers. They looked at each other all the while, some not-so-subtle currents resonating between them.

"I've never brought anyone else here," he said.

She glanced down at her glass, then met his gaze with a soft smile. "I'm glad," she said.

THE SUN HAD NEARLY RETIRED for the day, dusk laying strips of shadow across the pond.

Willa set down her wineglass, and reaching for the oars, began rowing.

"I'm impressed," Owen said.

"4-H camp."

"And some innate skill," he said while she continued to row with long, sure strokes to the far end of the pond. He couldn't take his eyes off her. Maybe it had been a crazy idea, coming here. There were certainly more impressive places he could have taken her.

He had never believed that there could really be one right woman for him. That he could look at her and just know it.

But sitting across from Willa in the old wooden boat, the truth of it was clear as day. He had met her. Felt the click. So it was true, after all.

GUYS HAD NEVER made Katie nervous.

That was her role. She'd always been the one to take a certain amount of pleasure in knowing she could shake up the opposite sex.

So what was the deal with all the butterflies in her stomach now?

She stood in front of the bathroom mirror, ran a brush through her hair again, then finally pulled it back in a ponytail. They were going to a party. No big deal. No point in acting like it was.

A few minutes later, she found Cline outside by the van waiting for her.

He smiled when she walked up. "Ready?" he asked.

"Yeah," she said. "How lame is this party going to be?"

"I think someone's bringing a new backgammon board. The Monopoly's always good, too."

Katie laughed. She stood by her door while he got himself into the minivan. It was hard to stand back and not help him. But that was the last thing he would have wanted, and she respected him for it.

Once they'd reached the main road, he glanced at her. "So did you go out a lot at home?"

"I pretty much majored in it. Do you? Go out a lot?"

Cline lifted one hand from the wheel. "I don't exactly fit the mold."

"What do you mean?"

"It's kind of hard to be cool at parties when you arrive in a butane-blue Dodge Caravan and then get out in a wheelchair."

The words were said without self-pity, but Katie heard the underlying seriousness. "I wish you could see yourself through my eyes."

He shot her a look.

She angled herself in the seat, hands splayed. "Here's what I see when I look at you. Great-looking. Cool clothes. Smart. Ten."

"And what about the van?" he asked with a smile.

Katie shrugged. "Wheels are always a plus."

His smile widened. He handed her a CD case and said, "Pick one."

"Any Mozart in here?" she asked, teasing.

"Would you be surprised if I said yes?"

"No," she said, giving him a level look of challenge. "He's not so bad, anyway."

WILLA SAT AT THE KITCHEN TABLE while Owen cooked.

He had insisted.

He pulled off the salad without a hitch.

Greens, diced sweet red pepper, goat cheese and an olive-oil balsamic dressing tossed in a heavy white bowl.

"I'm impressed," Willa said.

"Hold on," he said. "I haven't gotten to the main course yet."

Trout amandine. Smooth sailing here, too, until he got distracted by the search for a bread basket and let the almonds scorch.

By the time they sat down, white candles flickering at the center of the table, he looked less than certain of the meal's reception.

She took a bite of the salad. "Wonderful."

"Really?"

"Really. Where'd you learn to cook?"

He passed her the bread. "Living single. I have a very limited repertoire."

In spite of the burned almonds, which they mostly scraped aside, the trout was delicious.

When they were finished eating, they put their dishes in the sink.

"Dessert's a little more casual," Owen said. He picked up a brown paper bag, ushered her out onto the porch. Darkness had descended. A lone bird sang out in a melody of summer sound. Owen led her down to the dock where he had made a circle of rock, sticks piled high in the center.

He spread out the faded quilt, and they sat on it.

From the bag, he pulled a box of graham crackers, marshmallows and a couple of Hershey's candy bars.

"S'mores," she said.

He lit a match and tossed it on the sticks. "Katie kind of said you used to love them."

"I was once addicted," she said. And then added, "That's nice. That you asked her."

He smiled.

The flame poofed to life, and they sat on their knees next to it. Owen handed her a stick, the end whittled to a point. She picked up the marshmallows, stuck one on and held it over the fire.

They sat, silent, rotating the sticks until the marshmallows were toasty brown.

Willa pulled hers off, placed it between two crackers and added a piece of chocolate. She took a bite, closed her eyes. "So good." She looked up again to find him watching her.

He reached out then, touched a finger to the corner of her mouth. "Chocolate," he said.

"Oh," she said, wiping it with her thumb. "Did I get it?"

"Not quite." He leaned closer. "There. Gone."

He stayed where he was, his eyes holding hers.

She dropped her gaze, then ventured another look at him.

The night hung like a curtain around them, alive and talking.

"I love that sound," she said.

"Frogs."

She nodded. "When I was a girl, my grandparents had a farm. Katie and I spent a lot of weekends there with them. We camped out at the pond where the cows came for water. I can remember going to sleep in our tent, listening to them and the cows grazing out behind us."

"Good memory?"

Willa was silent for a moment. "It reminds me of being happy."

He brushed the back of his hand across her hair, a surprising tenderness in the gesture. "Are you now? Happy?"

"Oh. Well," she said, not meeting his eyes. "Yes. I am. Have been."

He tipped her chin up, forced her to look at him. "Really happy. Not just waiting to be happy."

She considered that, and then said, "There's a difference, isn't there?"

"Yeah. That bad experience you had?" he said, his voice low. "You've been holding on to that, haven't you?"

She didn't answer for a moment. "I guess I kind of have."

"Maybe it's time you let it go."

The fire popped and hissed. A spark landed on the ground beside them. Was he right? Had she put her own wants and needs on hold, as if one day the hurt would disappear, and suddenly she would trust again, let herself believe in someone?

Had she thought the pain would fade on its own, like a scar beneath the wear of time? She realized now her mistake. It wouldn't go away until she threw it away.

He put his hand on hers. She stared down at the connection. He turned his palm over, linked their fingers together, loose at first, and then closing tight.

They sat that way for a few moments while she considered her own questions about whether Owen's interest in her might be about his losing this farm. But then again, it wasn't as if he'd asked her to marry him.

He leaned in and kissed her, the taste of graham crackers and marshmallows sweet on their lips. And with that kiss, she decided this night was going to be about possibility. Her hand went to the side of his neck. He dropped the stick into the fire, looped an arm around her waist and settled her against him.

He cupped her face with both hands, deepening the kiss.

They stretched out on the quilt, turned on their sides, facing each other, kissed some more, his hand at the small of her back.

She ran her fingers through his hair, down the width of his shoulder, the hard muscles of his arm. And all the while, he kissed her, his touch suddenly as necessary as air. Making her wonder how she'd gone her whole life without it.

How was it a person could know in a single instant they had found the one? The one. For Willa, the answer was there in the way they fit against each other, in the way she felt completely alive beneath his touch.

The fire popped again, throwing up a shower of sparks.

Owen brushed the back of his hand across the hollow of her neck, slipped a thumb to the top button of her blouse, let it slip free from its snare. With his eyes, he asked permission. She closed her own, a silent answer. He dropped his mouth to the curve of her breast and kissed her there as if she were infinitely precious.

"You're beautiful, Willa."

She looked up at him. "It's not something I've ever cared about, but for now, for you, I'd like to be."

He said her name again low in his throat, kissed her full and deep. He rolled her to her back, then slid over her, stretched her arms above her head, entwined their fingers. He felt heavy and muscled in a distinctly pleasurable way.

Willa pulled back, hit with a sudden wave of self-consciousness. "Owen?"

He kissed the side of her jaw, worked his way to her ear. "Um?"

"I…it's been a long time since I…well."

He looked down at her, concern in his eyes. "Are you all right? Am I hurting you?"

She shook her head, made a short sound of laughter. "Ah, no. No." She put her hands to the side of his face, looked up at him. "I just want to get it right."

He bent his head to hers, kissed her with an intensity that made her think maybe she was. "I'm thinking you've got the hang of it," he said, teasing now.

"You're way too good at that," she said.

He smiled, pushed her hair back from her face. "Good as in smooth? Or good as in don't stop?"

"Definitely as in don't stop."

"Then I won't."

And he didn't.

A DOZEN OR MORE CARS were parked in the drive of the enormous brick colonial, home to Cline's friend Steve Matherson, whose parents were out of town for a week.

"Wow," Katie said. "Is anybody poor around here?"

Cline turned off the van and looked at her with a smile. "Don't let the trappings fool you. We have our share of screwups."

Katie got out of the van, waited for Cline to set up his chair, again resisting the urge to help.

Once he was settled, he waved her toward the house. "After you," he said.

The door opened before they reached the front step. A tall guy with a head full of blond hair loped down the steps and high-fived Cline. "Hey, man! Glad you could make it." He looked at Katie. "And this is?"

"Katie Addison. Katie, Steve Matherson."

"Hi," Katie said.

"You been keeping secrets, Miller?"

He held Katie's gaze for a second too long. She stepped closer to Cline's chair, glanced away.

Steve smiled. "Party's in the house. Need some help, Cline?"

"I got it. I'll meet you inside," he directed to Katie.

"Come on, Katie," Steve said, grabbing her hand. "I'll introduce you around."

Katie glanced after Cline who was already rolling down the sidewalk at one end of the house. "I'll go with—"

"He'll be fine," Steve said. "He always goes in that way. There's a ramp at the back. My grandmother lived with us for a while before she died."

It had not occurred to her that Cline couldn't go to just any party. That it would have to be one with a handicap entrance.

Somber-faced, she followed Steve inside, her heart feeling as if it were too big for her chest.

CHAPTER SEVENTEEN

WILLA LAY TUCKED in the curve of Owen's arm. He caressed her hair, kissed the top of her head.

"Are you okay?" he asked.

She nodded.

"If you're thinking I brought you up here with the intention of—"

"I'm not thinking that," she said.

They were quiet for a few moments. "Willa—"

She stopped him with a finger to his lips. "Remember what you said on the boat that afternoon?"

"Let it be," he said.

"Maybe that's what we should do about this. Just let it be what it is. Not expect it to be more."

He stroked her shoulder with one thumb, not wanting to agree, and yet unsure how to argue against it. With Willa in his arms, Owen finally knew what had been missing in his life. And he realized that he didn't want it to go on that way.

"There's something else," she said.

"What?"

"I've been thinking about what you said. About it not being too late for me."

"Yeah?"

"I'm thinking I might go back to school," she said a little self-consciously, as if he might find the idea ridiculous.

"Really?"

"The money Charles left me...I've been thinking about that, too. That maybe this is my chance to finish what I started. And to help Katie get an education as well, if she decides that's what she wants."

Owen let the words settle—maybe she was trying to tell him that what had just happened between them wouldn't go any further than tonight. "It's not crazy," he said. "And I can't imagine anything that would have made Charles happier."

"Do you think so?"

"I do." Owen tipped his head back, stared up at a sky full of stars.

"Tomorrow's your birthday," she said. "Cline mentioned it this morning."

"Yeah." So much to say, and yet not so much at all. He didn't want her to go. But what could he say now that wouldn't sound contrived? Wouldn't sound as if he had a deadline to meet? If he told her how he felt about her, how could he expect her to believe that it had nothing to do with the provision in his father's will?

She'd bought into something she'd thought was real once before and been disappointed in the worst possible way. How could he expect her to believe this was different? That he was different.

"I'm almost finished with the journals," she said now, her voice soft. "Katie and I will be heading back after that."

"Is that what you want?"

She hesitated, and then said, "It seems like the right thing."

But to Owen, nothing had ever felt more wrong.

CLINE SAT AT THE PERIMETER of the room, a bottle of Heineken in his right hand. Ice Cube was cranked on the music system, the bass making the ceiling-mounted speakers throb. Cline spotted Katie across the room. She waved once and smiled that smile that made him feel his balance was suddenly off.

He waved back, then started up an intense conversation about computers with a guy he didn't know. As soon as Katie looked away, Cline retreated to loner status.

Two hours into the party, and he was ready to leave.

It always went like this. People talked to him early on, and then he would end up on the sidelines, hanging out alone, trying to look like it didn't bother him.

Across the room, Katie smiled at something Steve had just said close to her ear. He touched a hand to her arm, and she laughed.

Cline watched them for another moment. He set the bottle on a nearby table, wheeled his chair through the house and out the back door.

OWEN TOOK THE OLD GREEN TRUCK back down the mountain in low gear. The headlights glanced off grazing deer, raccoons and an opossum.

The bench seat left only a couple of feet between them, and yet, to Willa, it already felt like miles.

"Owen?"

He glanced at her, one hand on the wheel.

"Are you sorry we came up here tonight?"

"No," he said. "Are you?"

"No." She paused. "But I'm not…this isn't usually…I don't—"

"I know," he said.

"So. In a day or two, I'll be going, and this will just—"

He looked at her again. "I don't think it will be that easy."

"Yeah," she said. What else was there to say?

KATIE WAS SO MAD at Cline, she could barely think around it.

He had left her at the party! Without saying a word!

And now she was being driven home by an intoxicated jerk with a real problem accepting no as an answer. No, she didn't want to go upstairs and see his bedroom. No, she wasn't an uptight prude.

Steve might have come in a more expensive package, but beneath the surface, he was no different from Eddie or any of the other losers she had dated in Pigeon Hollow.

A half-dozen beer cans rattled on the floorboard of the back seat.

It had been a mistake to get in the car with him. She knew that now. But when she'd found out Cline had left, any interest she'd had in staying at the party evaporated altogether.

Steve gunned the 911 engine and swung a hard right. She didn't know the roads here, but she remembered the turnoff that led back to Cline's.

She shot him a look of irritation. "Where are we going?"

"A little detour. What do you say?"

"I need to get back. Turn around, okay?"

"Easy, baby. It's no big deal if you're an hour

past your curfew. You don't turn into a pumpkin past midnight, do you?"

He laughed at this as if it were the funniest thing ever said.

Something like fear tickled at the pit of her stomach, only to be flooded by a tidal wave of anger. "Steve, turn the car around. Or pull over, and I'll walk."

He ignored her, shifting into a lower gear and gunning the engine. They flew down a straight stretch of road, took a sudden curve too fast. Katie felt the car give, on the verge of flipping, and then right itself at the last moment.

"Steve, stop the car!"

He hit the brake, turning off the main road onto a narrow dirt lane. They bumped along for a quarter mile or so, until he stopped and cut the engine.

"Let me out, Steve," she said. "I'll walk back."

He turned in the seat, put a hand on her shoulder. "What's the big deal?"

She gave him a glacier glare. "The big deal is I don't want to be here."

He smiled a knowing smile. "Katie, I know plenty of girls like you. Let's cut through the bullshit. You've been playing the innocent all night. When we both know that's not who you are."

The words struck somewhere deep inside her.

Was that how Cline saw her? Was that why he had left? "You have no idea who I am."

"Yeah? How's this?"

He leaned over, kissed her hard, one hand at the back of her neck. His tongue stabbed into her mouth, and she lunged backward, banging her head on the window. An explosion of stars went off behind her closed eyes.

She struggled, pushing at his chest.

"You want to play like that, huh?"

His eyes were narrow, and there was a meanness in their depths she didn't know how she could have missed earlier.

He lay half-across her, holding her shoulders down while his mouth ground against hers. Revulsion thickened in her throat. She was going to be sick.

Had she done something to deserve this? Somehow asked for it? Made herself out to be a girl he could use and throw away?

It hit her then that was exactly who she had once been. Who she had set herself up to be. Someone to be discarded. Left behind.

But she didn't want to be that person anymore. She thought about Cline and the way she felt smart around him, as if she could go places and do things she'd never imagined herself capable of doing.

The old Katie was someone she never wanted to be again. The new Katie wanted more.

She let her mouth go slack for a moment, no longer resisting. She felt his surprise, the kiss changing tack like a sail to a wind from a different direction. One second, two seconds, three… she bit into his lower lip, hard.

He yelped, and in that instant, she reached between his legs, grabbed dead center and twisted as hard as she could.

He let out a yowl of pain. "Bitch!"

Katie fumbled for the door lock, popped it up and fell out of the car. She scrambled on her hands and knees, gravel piercing her palms.

She glanced over her shoulder. Steve opened the car door and rolled out, cussing. "Come back here!"

She got to her feet, stumbled over a tree root and nearly fell. She plunged down the dark road, found her footing and ran as fast as she could go.

OKAY, CLINE WAS way beyond worried.

He glanced at the grandfather clock in the foyer. One-thirty. And still, Katie wasn't back.

He'd called Steve's house just after midnight. Some drunk girl had said they'd left hours ago.

Steve was a big ladies' man. Had slept with half the girls in their class. Or so he said. Katie had seemed pretty into him.

Maybe they were just out somewhere having a good time.

But something didn't feel right about it.

Cline had left her at that party. If something happened to her…

He rolled his chair to the door. He had to find her.

OWEN STOPPED THE TRUCK at the side of the house next to Cline's van. He got out and opened Willa's door, waited for her to slide to the ground.

Cline lowered his window, the engine running.

"It's awful late," Owen said. "You coming or going?"

"Katie's not home yet," Cline said, his face set.

A ping of alarm went off inside Willa. "Where is she?"

Cline looked uneasy, and then admitted, "I don't know. I left before she did. I called back out there a little while ago. Someone said she had left with Steve, the guy throwing the party. I thought I'd go look for them."

Willa glanced at her watch. Nearly 2:00 a.m. "We'll come with you," she said, starting to feel panicky.

Owen put a hand on her arm. "Maybe we should stay here in case she comes home or someone calls."

Fear sliced through Willa's chest. A dozen explanations for Katie's being late sailed through her thoughts, each one worse than the former. "Okay," she said.

"Got your cell phone?" Owen asked Cline.

Cline nodded. "I'll call when I catch up with her."

"Thanks," Willa said.

She and Owen walked in the house where Sam offered up an ecstatic welcome. Willa bent down and rubbed his back. They went into the kitchen. Owen made some coffee and poured her a cup.

"I can see your imagination working overtime," he said. "I'm sure she's fine."

Willa blew out a sigh. "I had begun to think we might be past this."

Owen sat down in the chair beside her and set his coffee cup on the table. "It's probably not what you think. But even if it is, big brother speaking to a big sister here, you're not going to be able to prevent her from making mistakes."

Willa ran a hand through her hair, kneaded the back of her neck where stress had instantly drawn the muscles in knots. "I just want good things for her."

"I know," he said. He was silent for a moment, and then said, "A year or so after Cline's accident, he got into some pretty bad stuff. For a long time,

I thought he wanted to kill himself. Maybe he did. I tried everything I knew to turn him around, but in the end, he had to decide for himself."

"He seems like such a levelheaded kid."

"He is. Now. I guess my point is sometimes there are just places we have to get to by ourselves."

"I know," she said softly. The ironic thing was the words applied just as easily to her as they did to Katie.

KATIE HAD NO IDEA how many miles she'd walked.

Her sandals had rubbed a blister between her toes. The balls of her feet ached. She had to pee really bad.

She'd passed a small country store with a pay phone out front, but she'd left her purse in Steve's car. And pride or stubbornness had refused to let her call Cline's house collect.

A truck with a hole in the muffler roared past, hit the brakes and backed up, tires screeching to a stop right beside her.

"Hey, sweet thing." The driver was bald, late-forties, with a gold-capped tooth that glinted in the dark. "You need a ride?"

"I'm fine, thanks," she said and walked on.

The truck idled along beside her. She could smell the alcohol on his breath from ten feet away.

"Come on. I don't bite."

The very thought was enough to turn her stomach. Katie darted up the bank into a cornfield.

The truck roared off, a string of bad language sailing out the window, tires smoking.

Katie bit back a sob and started running.

CLINE ARRIVED BACK at Steve's house to find the red 911 parked in the driveway.

He opened the lift and got out of the van. Rolled around back and made his way through the house. The remaining guests were mostly passed out on the stairs, the living room floor.

Steve was still at it, putting the moves on a younger girl Cline recognized from school who looked as if she could barely hold her head up.

Cline rolled up behind them. "Sorry to interrupt," he said, not sounding sorry at all.

Steve swung around, a frown on his face.

"Where's Katie?"

"How should I know?"

"You left with her, didn't you?"

"So what if I did?"

"So you better tell me where she is."

"Like it matters. And by the way, thanks for the warning, buddy," he said, sarcasm etched in the words. "That one was a waste of time."

Cline blinked back a wave of rage. "I'm going to ask you one more time. Where is she?"

"Probably back at your house by now. It wasn't that long a walk."

"You moron," Cline said in a low voice.

Steve shot him a look of annoyance, as if he were a fly that had been pestering him too long.

Cline balled his fists, stared at him through narrowed eyes. He swung his chair around and wheeled out the way he'd come in.

Outside, he opened the side door to his van, rummaged through the glove compartment, pulled out a leather case.

He unsnapped it, slid out the knife he kept there for emergencies. He rolled across the grass to the 911, sat for a moment, considering how best to make his point.

He started with the left front tire, sliced a straight gash from the twelve o'clock position to the three o'clock. The air released with a satisfying sigh. Cline moved to the back and repeated the same cut. And then again. And again. Until Steve's chick magnet sat flat on the ground.

THE PHONE RANG at just after three.

Owen saw the look of panic in Willa's eyes, squeezed her shoulder once, then picked up the cordless. "Hello."

Silence, and then quiet weeping from the other end.

"Katie?"

"Yeah," she said, the word barely audible.

"Are you all right? Where are you?"

"In a dairy barn. There was a phone just inside the door here."

"Are you okay?"

She sniffled and said something that sounded like yes.

"Can you look around? See if there's anything with an address?"

"There's a milk crate by the phone. The label on the side says Olden's Dairy."

"Carter Olden. I know where you are. Stay put, Katie. We'll come and get you."

"Okay," she said and hung up.

CHAPTER EIGHTEEN

THEY MADE IT to the Olden's Dairy in less than fifteen minutes, Owen not cutting the speed limit any slack. He called Cline on his cell phone and let him know they were going to get Katie.

A short gravel drive wound from the main road down to the house and dairy. Black-and-white Holstein cows stood in a line at one end of the barn, waiting for milking time.

Katie waited just outside the entrance, arms folded across her chest, her gaze on the ground.

Owen turned off the engine and said, "Sam and I will wait here."

"Thanks." Willa got out of the Rover and walked the few steps to where Katie waited. "Hi," she said.

"Hi." Katie looked up then, her face set.

"What happened?" Willa asked softly, not sure she wanted to hear the answer.

Katie sat down on the concrete steps outside the barn, propped her arms on her knees and buried her face in her hands, silent.

Willa waited, feeling her sister's struggle to find words.

Finally, Katie turned her head and said, "I didn't mean for it to happen."

"Tell me about it?"

Katie's white teeth pulled at her lower lip. "Do I look like an easy target?"

Willa took in her sister's soft pink sundress, her short blond ponytail, now-scuffed white sandals. Saw the way she had bloomed during their time here. "No," she said.

Tears welled in Katie's eyes, slid down her cheeks.

Something snapped in Willa's heart, and she reached for her sister, pulling her tight up against her, kissing the top of her head. "I'm sorry," she said. "Not just for what happened to you tonight, but for the things that weren't the way they should have been when we were growing up. I'd give anything to take all that away from you, Katie."

Katie wrapped her arms around Willa's waist, buried her face in her shoulder and sobbed. They sat that way for a good while until her sobs softened, her breathing even. "None of it was your fault, Willa. I know I've tried to put the blame on you, but I was wrong to do it. I'm sorry for that."

"Shh." Willa smoothed Katie's hair. "All that

anger? Maybe it was just a bridge to get to where we are now. And right here is a great place to be."

Katie pulled back, looked up at her through eyes still wet with tears. "You always accept me, no matter how awful I am."

"That's because I love you. And that's what love is. Although I have to say, I really like this Katie." She hesitated, and then said, "There's something I want to tell you."

"What?"

"Charles…my father. He left me quite a bit of money."

Surprise registered on Katie's face. "How much is quite a bit?"

"Actually, it's two million dollars."

Katie stared at Willa, her eyes wide now, amazed. "Wow."

"I know. It's crazy. Reading his journals, I discovered that he wanted to be a doctor."

"Like you."

"It kind of freaked me out when I read it. But since we've been here, I've done a lot of thinking. Katie, I wanted to do the right thing by you. Be the family you needed. Somewhere in all that, I lost sight of the life I had intended to pursue. And I think maybe you haven't respected me for that."

Katie looked down at her hands, rubbed a thumb across one palm. "I don't deserve you."

Willa reached out, tilted her chin up, forcing her to look at her. "We're sisters. We deserve each other."

Katie laughed. "There's probably some truth in that. So. Are you gonna go back to school?"

"Yeah," she said, smiling. "I think I might."

Katie nodded. "Good. We could use a doctor in the family."

"And you? When we get home, what's the verdict on school?"

Katie looked down at the ground, then straight into Willa's eyes. "I'm thinking I'd like to make something of myself."

"Oh, Katie," Willa said, her throat suddenly tight. "Then you will."

A light flicked on from the front porch at the house. A man in bib overalls stepped out, peering toward the barn. Owen got out of the Rover, walked up to greet him, calling his name. The man stopped, and they began to talk.

Katie glanced at the two men. "What about you and Owen?"

Willa dropped her gaze. "I'm not sure what to think about that."

"You're not going to let something that good go, are you?"

Willa glanced back at Owen, her gaze settling on his wide shoulders, the memory of everything they'd shared tonight already imprinted upon her like a permanent tattoo beneath the skin. "Sometimes," she said, "it's hard to be sure something is real."

"Sometimes," Katie said, "it's hard to be sure it isn't."

WHEN THEY GOT back to the house, Cline was waiting by the front door. Katie glanced at him, then ran upstairs without speaking.

Cline wheeled around and headed for his room.

Owen started to call him back, stopped, then looked at Willa. "Any idea what that's all about?"

"No, but they'll get it worked out, I'm sure," she said.

He nodded, watched her for a moment. "What a night."

"Yeah."

"You must be tired."

"I'm just glad everything is all right."

"Me, too."

She glanced down at her hands, then met his gaze. "Thanks, Owen. For taking me to the cabin. For the dinner. And everything."

"Thanks for going."

They stood, awkward, uncertain.

"Well, good night," she said.

"Good night."

She started up the stairs.

"Willa?"

She turned, looked back.

"Tonight was—" He broke off there, left the rest hanging.

"It was," she said. It really was.

KATIE LAY IN BED, staring at the ceiling.

It was nearly morning. Going to sleep seemed a waste of effort.

She rolled over onto her side, punched her pillow. Closed her eyes and started counting.

She flopped back over, eyes wide open.

She let out a loud sigh. She couldn't quit thinking about that look on Cline's face when she'd come through the door a little while ago. He was mad at her. That much was impossible to miss.

Which really pissed her off. She was the one who should be mad at him. He had left her at the party and never even said a word!

She flung herself out of bed, pulled on a pair of jeans with the T-shirt doubling as a nightgown. She marched down the stairs and followed the hall to Cline's first-floor bedroom, rapped on the door.

No answer. She turned the knob and stuck her head inside. "Cline?"

He raised up on one elbow. "Katie? What are you doing?"

"I need to talk to you."

"Can't it wait until morning?"

"It is morning. And no, it can't."

"I'm in bed in case you hadn't noticed."

"I did," she said, crossing the floor to sit down on the corner of the mattress. It was hard to look at him, now that she was actually here in his bedroom. Also hard not to.

His wheelchair sat by the bed's headboard.

"What is it?" he asked.

She managed to look at him then, stared hard. His chest was bare, the muscles there surprisingly pronounced. "Why did you take off like that?" she finally asked, her voice rusty in her throat.

"You noticed?"

"Yeah, I noticed."

He lifted a shoulder. "You seemed pretty into Matherson."

Katie let that stand for a moment. "Well, you had the wrong impression."

"Oh, I did?"

"You did."

They looked at each other for several seconds, Katie's heart thrumming.

"I'm guessing Matherson got a little out of line," Cline said.

"A little."

His smile disappeared. "He's going to have some trouble getting out of his driveway today."

Katie raised an eyebrow. "Did you go back out there?"

"I did."

The sky outside Cline's window had begun to lighten. He had taken up for her. Emotion tightened her chest. She looked down at her hands and said, "You didn't have to do that."

"I was worried about you."

She glanced up at him and smiled. Again, they stared at each other, attraction crackling between them like stray lightning. He leaned forward, one hand cupping the side of her face.

She bolted back, holding up one hand. "Just a minute, okay?"

"Where are you going?"

She didn't answer, just tore down the hall and up the stairs to her bathroom where she grabbed her toothbrush and toothpaste, brushed, rinsed and spit at an Olympic-relay pace.

She ran back down the stairs, down the hall, skidding to a stop beside the bed. "Where were we?"

Cline smiled, reached for her hand and pulled her down beside him. "Right here."

THAT MORNING, WILLA SAT in the kitchen finishing up the last of the journals. The final page had been written on the day Owen arrived in Pigeon Hollow.

An enormous favor to ask, I know. Owen is a good man to do this for me. Don't know how much time I have left, but I don't want my life to end without meeting my daughter. It's such a long road, this life. So hard to look ahead when we're far from the final destination. But this is the one thing I would have taught her. To weed out the insignificant, look for what's really important. To love and be loved. In the end, that's all that matters.

Willa closed the journal, sat with her hand on the cover, her throat tight. When she'd first learned of her father's existence, she couldn't have imagined that she would ever feel anything other than bitterness for the fact that he had not been a part of her life.

The bitterness was gone now. In its place, something that felt like acceptance. And, too, gratitude. In coming to Lexington, she had followed a road that was opening up a future she had not thought possible.

For the first time in so long, she wanted to be the woman she had once dreamed of being. She wouldn't change a thing she had done for Katie. She and Katie were sisters again. And it was nice to think that she could be there for her without giving up the things she wanted as well.

And there was Owen.

Owen.

She didn't regret last night. How could she regret something that made her feel as if she'd found a missing piece of herself?

For so long, she had feared that Katie would let her hurt over their mother's rejection take over the rest of her life. But wasn't that exactly what she had been doing as well by shutting herself off to dating, to the possibility of meeting someone who might be worthy of her trust? And, too, in putting aside her dreams? Deciding not to reach for fear of the fall.

Owen had opened a door for her. And it wasn't so scary on the other side. Willa realized now that she had let the setbacks in her life determine her future, that circumstance would toss you around if you let it. But no matter what happened—if what she and Owen had found ceased to exist once she left here—then she would still be the same person. A woman who had finally given herself permission to go after her own dreams.

And if those feelings did have a place, well… Well.

CLINE ROLLED INTO THE KITCHEN just as Willa was putting her coffee cup in the sink. "Hey," he said.

"Hey."

He opened the refrigerator, pulled out a gallon of milk. "Katie said you're leaving tomorrow."

Willa nodded. "I'd say we've used up the welcome mat."

Cline set the milk on the table, a frown creasing his forehead. "Since you and Katie came here, this house has been alive in a way it hasn't in a really long time."

Something in his voice made Willa's heart contract. "Thank you, Cline."

"Actually, I wanted to thank you." He hesitated, and then said, "You and Owen—"

She heard the question behind the words, didn't know what to say. "Maybe it's a case of wrong place, wrong time."

"Is there such a thing, or is that just what people say when they don't know how to see something for what it really is?"

Willa thought about those last words her father had written. To weed out the insignificant. Look for what's really important. "You're not supposed to be this wise at seventeen."

Cline smiled at that. "I thought Owen could use a party since it's his birthday. Think you could help me throw something together for him tonight?"

"I'd be happy to," she said.

AFTER LEAVING THE HOUSE, Cline wheeled his chair down to the barn. He found Jake in the tack room oiling a saddle. "You seen Owen?"

"He's in the office."

"Thanks."

Cline rolled down the aisle, stopped halfway and knocked on the closed door.

"Come in."

Cline swung it open, wheeled inside. "Just me," he said.

Owen sat at the desk, a stack of papers in front of him. He waved him in. "What's up?"

Cline looked down at his hands, then said, "I shouldn't have left Katie at that party last night."

Owen watched him for a moment. "Probably not."

"I was so busy thinking about myself, I didn't think about her."

"We've all been guilty of that," Owen said, his voice softening.

Cline was silent a moment. "Is that kind of what you're doing with Willa?"

Owen sat back in his chair, his expression giving nothing away. "What do you mean?"

"Clearly, you're crazy about her."

Owen picked up the pencil on the desk, tapped the point against the stack of papers in front of him. "In this case, I don't think that would be enough."

"But how do you know?"

Owen released a sigh. "I've never met a woman I wanted to spend my life with until now. And here I am, either get married or lose this place. How could she believe my wanting her has nothing to do with any of that?"

"Have you told her that?"

He shook his head. "No."

"So you're just going to toss it all out the window?"

He hesitated, and then said, "I'm going to tell her how I feel about her. Tonight. After midnight."

Cline's gaze widened. "But then you'll lose the farm. And Dad will win."

"It'll go to you, Cline. There's nothing lost in that."

He threw up his hands. "Even if I have other things I want to do with my life?"

"I'm not telling you what you should do with it. That'll be up to you."

Cline glanced away, then met his brother's gaze. "Sometimes I think this has been your intention all along. That you want me to have this place out of guilt."

"Cline—" Owen began.

"You didn't cause this to happen to me, Owen,"

he interrupted, pointing at his legs. "I know I've been kind of a jerk lately. But if I've directed it at you, it's only because for whatever stupid reason, people take stuff out on the ones they love the most."

It was the closest he'd ever come to telling his brother he loved him. Sudden gratitude shone in Owen's eyes.

"Whatever happens," Owen said, "nothing's going to change between us. Dad had his reasons for what he did, and I guess to him they made sense. But you and me? We'll always be on the same page, okay?"

Cline stopped himself from arguing further. He knew his brother, and Owen had made up his mind about which way he was going with this.

This particular track was a dead-end road. Which meant he had to find another way in.

HE STARTED with Louisa.

"Well, of course, we can do a party for Owen's birthday," she said, wiping her hands on her apron. "I wish we'd thought of it sooner, so we could have it today."

"Tonight," Cline said. "Could we have it to-night?"

"Tonight? But how on earth—"

"It's really important, Louisa. Willa said she'll help. And I know Katie will. Please?"

She gave him the same look she gave him for snacking too close to supper, then said, "Tonight it is."

Cline popped her a kiss. "Thanks, Louisa!"

She waved him away, blushing.

He flew out of the kitchen then, tires whooshing against the wood floor.

JAKE'S ROLE WAS TO GET Owen out of the house for the rest of the day. He faked a virus and asked Owen to make the two-hour drive to pick up some papers for a mare being shipped out of the country later that evening.

Owen called the house and asked Willa to go with him. With Louisa smiling in the background, she said, "I promised Natalie I would come by this afternoon." Which, technically, was true.

"How about dinner tonight?"

"Okay," she said.

"I'll be back around eight. Is that too late?"

"No," she said. "I'll see you then."

The house was busier than a beehive for the rest of the day. Everyone pitched in, taking a role. Cline worked the phone, making up a list and placing calls.

Willa, Louisa and Katie cooked. They made an enormous sheet cake, slathered it with chocolate icing, which Cline said was Owen's favorite. Willa made bite-size ham biscuits; Katie made choco-late-chip cookies (Cline's favorite); Louisa put to-gether a huge tray of finger sandwiches, pimento cheese and chicken salad.

Jake hung balloons and streamers in the living room and on the terrace.

Midafternoon, Cline rolled into the flour-strewn kitchen, waving a notepad. "Any last-min-ute suggestions for invites?"

Katie opened the refrigerator, put away the eggs and milk. "What about Judy?"

"Is she the one who's taking care of your diner?" Cline asked.

"Yeah," Katie said. "What do you think, Willa?"

"If it's okay with Cline," Willa said. "I'd love for her to come."

Cline waved a hand. "Sure it is."

"I don't know how she'd feel about driving," Willa said, thinking of Judy's old car.

Jake walked into the kitchen. "Where is she? I'll be glad to go pick her up."

Willa smiled at Jake. "I think she'll be giving me extra credit for this assignment."

CHAPTER NINETEEN

OWEN PARALLEL PARKED the farm truck in front of a stretch of high-end retail stores. He got out, went inside the discreet entrance to Beckman's Jewelers.

A black-clad salesclerk frowned at him from behind the counter, her hair pulled back in a bun so tight it made slits of her eyes. He glanced down at his dirt-splattered blue jeans and muddy boots, then shot her a wide smile, deliberately keeping it blank of apology.

"May I help you with something, sir?" she asked without looking at him, power-buffing a thumbnail with an emery board.

"Yes," he said, pointing at the center of the case where the largest rings were displayed. "I'm hoping you can."

Her eyes widened. She dropped the nail file in a drawer, popped it closed. "Indeed," she said.

KATIE HAD HUNG THE LAST of the streamers across the terrace doorway when Cline waved for her to follow him. Willa and Louisa were in deep discussion over where to place the cake table. Katie got down from the ladder and jogged after Cline.

He turned into Owen's office, waited for her to step inside and then closed the door. "So here's the deal. Owen thinks if he asks Willa to marry him while it's still his birthday, there's no way she'll ever believe it had nothing to do with the inheritance."

"Does it?"

"I've never seen my brother in love. Owen's in love."

Katie smiled at that, proud somehow that it was her sister who had come along in time to turn that around with a hunk like Owen. "Can I ask you something?"

"Sure."

"Why would you do all this when you're the one who inherits everything if Owen doesn't get engaged?"

Cline shrugged, glancing out the window behind the desk. "Maybe because I think deep down he believes if he lets all this revert to me, it will somehow make up for where I am. For whatever part he thinks he played in it."

"Would it?" she asked softly.

He paused, then said, "No. At some point, I finally figured out that holding a grudge doesn't work for anybody. Least of all me."

The conviction in Cline's voice stirred a well of admiration inside her. "Anyone ever told you you're amazing?"

Cline looked up at her. "Not recently," he said.

"You're amazing."

He smiled at her. "So," he said. "I've got a plan."

She smiled back. "I never doubted that."

ONCE THEY'D FINISHED with all the decorating, Willa and Katie borrowed Cline's van and drove into Lexington to buy something to wear.

At Louisa's recommendation, they went to a different shop than the one they'd gone to when they'd first arrived at Owen's.

Annabelle's carried a nice eclectic mix, funky enough for Katie, a little more mainstream for Willa.

The salesclerk left them to browse. Willa pulled a dark blue dress from the rack, held it up for Katie to see.

She gave an adamant headshake followed by, "Too Queen Mother."

Willa laughed.

Katie riffled through a smaller rack, stopped, flipped past and then yanked one out, holding it up with a wide smile. "This one."

The dress looked like nothing Willa had ever worn. "I'm not sure," she said.

"Just try it on."

Reluctant, Willa took the dress inside the fitting room, shrugged out of her jeans and slipped it on. She came back out, stood in front of the mirror.

Pale blue with skinny straps and a fitted waist, she had to admit it was flattering.

Katie grinned, clapped her hands together. "That's it."

"It's beautiful," Willa said. "I'm just not sure it's me."

"Judy always says when you've found the perfect thing, it's time to quit looking."

"Except that I think her context was men."

Katie smiled a mischievous smile. "Who said mine wasn't?"

JAKE PULLED INTO THE DRIVEWAY with Judy at the same time Willa and Katie got back from shopping.

At the sight of them, Willa jumped out and ran to Jake's truck.

Judy slid out of the passenger side, wrapping her in a warm hug. "If you aren't a sight for sore eyes."

"Oh, you, too, Judy," Willa said. "I'm so glad you could come."

Jake got out of the truck and helped Katie with the bags she pulled from the van.

"Well, me, too," she said, glancing up at the house and surrounding pastures. "Wow."

"Yeah," Willa said. "I owe you so much for taking care of the diner for me."

Judy shot a glance at Jake. "I think you just managed to pay me back."

Willa looked at Jake and smiled. "Oh."

Jake turned his gaze on Judy.

She instantly blushed.

"It was my pleasure," he said.

BY EIGHT-FIFTEEN, Owen still wasn't home.

Cline had directed everyone to park behind the barn so the cars wouldn't be visible. The living room overflowed with guests, neighbors and business associates, some of Cline's friends from school, all sipping the punch Louisa had made with a secret recipe so good she fairly beamed from all the compliments.

Just when everyone began to think Owen wasn't coming, Cline said, "He's here! Places!"

Katie giggled and rolled her eyes.

Willa smiled, and they both ducked behind the foyer doorway. The house was so quiet they could hear Owen's footsteps on the walkway outside.

He opened the door, stepped in and flipped on the light.

"Surprise!" The house full of people exploded all at once. Sam barked his own greeting, running circles.

Owen braced a hand in the doorway and then smiled. He searched the crowd now milling in the foyer, his gaze settling on Willa. They stared at each other for a long moment.

"Happy birthday," she said.

He crossed the floor, stopping in front of her. "Now it is."

OWEN HAD TO GIVE IT to his little brother. He knew how to pull off a party. Cline had confessed the whole thing had been last minute, and yet there wasn't a single thing to indicate it hadn't been weeks in the making.

A buddy of Cline's—headed for Juilliard on scholarship—played the piano. The upbeat repertoire of everything from Hank Williams Jr. to Josh Groban had the whole room dancing.

Owen had spent the first hour of the party making small talk with guests. The entire time he was aware of Willa, her smile, her laughter, that incredible dress she was wearing. He could barely take his eyes off her.

They finally arrived at the same spot in the room. He put a hand on her elbow and said, "May I have this dance?"

She looked up at him and smiled. "What if I step on your toes?"

He grinned. "No cake for you."

"Oh, and it's such great cake."

He opened his arms, and she stepped into them.

KATIE AND CLINE stood at the edge of the room, watching Owen and Willa dance.

"If they don't look like they should be together, who does?"

Jake and Judy danced by. Katie peered around them. "It is kind of sickening, isn't it? To look at them, you'd think there wasn't anyone else in the room."

"Ready for phase two of Operation Owen-Willa?"

"Ready and willing, sir."

"Okay. Let's move in."

OWEN DIPPED WILLA across his left arm, barely resisting the urge to kiss the arch of her neck.

"Okay, that's enough of that."

He brought Willa, laughing, back to an upright position. They both turned to find Katie giving them a look that belonged on the face of a mother with teenagers out past curfew.

"Sorry," Owen said, trying to sound like he meant it.

"Cline wants to know if he can borrow your watch for a minute. His broke this afternoon, and he keeps asking everyone what time it is. Louisa's got him watching a batch of cookies."

Owen took off his watch, handed it to her. "Ah, sure."

"I'll bring it back in a few minutes," Katie said.

And if Owen thought the request a little curious, he forgot about it as soon as he turned his attention back to the woman in his arms.

AT ELEVEN O'CLOCK, Cline and Katie met in front of the oversize grandfather clock in the far corner of the living room.

They'd had to bring Jake and Judy in on the gig because they needed them to stand in front of the clock so Cline could make the adjustment without the whole room turning around to look.

He moved the oversize hand, then quickly closed the door, looked at Katie and grinned. "Done," he said.

She smiled back. "Done."

THE CLOCK STRUCK twelve. Sean hit the last few notes of a Jill Scott favorite.

Owen stopped dancing, looked down at Willa.

"It's midnight," she said.

He brushed the back of his hand across her hair. "Yeah."

"You're not sad?" she asked.

"About what?"

"The provision in your father's will."

He studied her for a moment, and then asked, "Come outside for a minute?"

"Okay," she said, wondering why he hadn't answered her question.

He led her through the mingling guests onto the terrace.

Above, the sky was perfectly clear, stars scattered like diamonds. They walked over to the rock wall, looked out at the barn and the fields beyond.

"What a great night," Willa said.

"Having you here, it's been amazing." His voice was low, sincere.

She looked up, met his eyes. "Being here has changed my life, Owen. Literally."

He reached for her hand, laced his fingers through hers. "I used to think there would never be anyone I could feel this way about. That for me, the real thing just didn't exist. That everybody else was making it up."

Willa's heart beat a steady drum at the base of her throat.

"And then you came along, and nothing looks the way it used to look."

She stared at him. "What are you saying, Owen?"

"I'm saying," he said softly, "my little brother is right. I'm crazy about you, Willa."

She tried to speak, couldn't find the words. Finally, she managed to say, "Owen, I—"

He pointed at his watch. "Ten past midnight. I'm thirty-three. And no longer the owner of Winding Creek Farm."

Understanding hit her in a wave. "You waited until after midnight—"

"Yeah," he said.

She shook her head. "Why?"

"So you would believe me when I say what I feel for you is real. It's real, Willa."

"Owen," she said, her voice raspy with disbelief.

He kissed her then, a long sweet kiss. When he pulled back, he slid a hand in the pocket of his jacket, removed a black velvet box.

She stared at it, eyes wide.

He opened it. A very large diamond solitaire winked up at her. "Will you marry me, Willa?"

She put a hand to her mouth, no idea what to say.

He reached out, touched her face. "We can take all the time you want. We don't have to do the wedding thing now. I just want us to be together."

Less than two weeks ago, Willa had been certain she would never find the magic she had once believed in. And yet, in front of her stood a man who had not only made her believe in it, but want it for herself as well.

Love and be loved. In the end, it is all that matters. These were the words her father had left her. All that matters.

"I don't know," she said. "I've always been a church-and-flowers kind of girl."

Owen smiled, leaned in and kissed her soundly, cupping her face with his hands. "Is that a yes?"

"That's a yes," she said and kissed him back.

A LITTLE LATER, they went inside to tell Cline and Katie the news. The two teenagers hovered by the terrace door, looking as if they were harboring national secrets.

Owen put his arm around Willa, tucked her close. "We have something to tell you," he said.

"What?" Cline and Katie both yelped in unison.

Owen looked at Willa and smiled. She raised her hand, the diamond ring glinting.

"Oh, my gosh!" Katie leaped into her sister's arms, hugging her hard.

Cline pumped Owen's hand in congratulations, a broad smile on his face.

Jake and Judy stepped forward, both wearing expectant expressions.

"They did it," Cline said, grinning at Jake.

Jake clapped Owen on the shoulder. "It's about time you settled down with a good woman."

Cline's smile grew wider. He looked at Katie. "What time do you have, Katie?"

Katie held her watch up, gave it a steady perusal. "Ten to midnight."

Owen frowned, looked at his watch, shot a glance at the grandfather clock across the room. "Cline," he said.

Cline held up a hand, pointed at Art Travers who stood next to Jake, smiling.

"Witness to the fact," the attorney said. "Looks like you got yourself engaged before midnight. Provision met."

Owen looked at Cline, shaking his head. "You changed my watch."

Cline did a poor imitation of shocked and bewildered. Katie's wasn't much better.

Owen looked at Willa. "We've been duped."

"By a couple of experts, it would seem," she said, smiling.

Someone grabbed a couple bottles of champagne. Cline popped one cork. Katie, the other. Sam barked. And the celebrating began.

EPILOGUE

THE LITTLE GIRL ASTRIDE the kind-eyed bay mare wore a smile as wide as the saddle on which she sat perched. She had long dark hair, braided into a ponytail that hung down the center of her back. "Can we go round one more time, Katie?" she asked.

Katie patted the mare on the neck, led her on past the white gate and said, "Sure, we can. I think Delilah will be sad when you're done, anyway. I can tell she likes you very much."

"Really?" The little girl brightened. "How?"

"Well, her ears are forward, which means she's happy. And every time she hears your voice, one ear flicks back to listen."

If possible, the little girl's smile grew wider. "When I get big, I want to work at a summer camp just like you, Katie."

Katie rubbed the mare's neck, a pleased smile touching her lips. "Who knows, maybe you can work at this one."

Willa took in the conversation from outside the ring where she and Owen stood watching. Tears sprung to her eyes. She wiped them away with the back of her hand. Owen put his arm around her shoulders, kissed her temple.

"Sometimes I look at her," Willa said after a few moments, "and I can't believe she's the same girl she was a few months ago."

"She's happy with herself. It shows."

Willa smiled. "It does, doesn't it?"

At the far end of the ring, Cline rolled up to the gate, opened it and waited for Katie to lead the mare through. He handed her a bottle of water, said something to the little girl who all but beamed with pride. He beckoned Katie close then, spoke into her ear. She giggled, gave him a playful thwack on the shoulder.

Laughter rang up from the outdoor wash stall. Jake and Judy had been hosing off one of the geldings who was done for the day. It looked as though Judy had turned the hose on Jake, and they were wrestling over the nozzle, a geyser of water shooting straight up and showering back down on them both.

Sam ran circles around them, barking and wagging his tail.

Owen reached for Willa's hand. "Nice, isn't it?"

"Very. I'm glad now that Clara and her husband

are buying the diner. I thought for a while it might be the right thing for Judy, but it's looking like she might end up here in Lexington."

"If Jake has anything to do with it," Owen said with a knowing look.

Willa glanced up at him, her heart so full she wondered at times if it could hold all the happiness she felt. "I wish the camp didn't have to end," she said. "It's been so much fun."

"We'll do it again next year." He turned her to face him, kissing the tip of her nose and then her lips, pulling back to look down at her with a deep satisfaction in his eyes. "And besides, we've got a wedding to pull off."

"Oh, yeah, that," she said, flip.

He'd long since discovered her ticklish spots, made use of them now until she collapsed with laughter, begging for a reprieve.

"A wedding," she said, breathless. "I'll get right on it."

He pulled her to him then, kissed her soundly, until her arms went around his neck, and she kissed him back, hands cupping his face.

"So," he said, forehead pressed to hers, breathing less than steady. "Wedding in two weeks. One week on a yet-to-be disclosed Caribbean island, and then you're off to college."

"Sounds a little crazy, doesn't it?"

"University of Kentucky, here she comes."

Willa put a hand to the center of his chest, felt his still-pounding heart beneath her hand. "Thank you."

"For what?"

"For understanding about my dreams."

He ran the back of his hand across her hair. "Isn't that what we all owe ourselves? To decide what it is we want out of this life and do our best to make it happen. You? You're going to make most of your dreams come true all by yourself." He leaned in, kissed the side of her neck, said in a voice only she could hear, "I'd like to think I might have a chance at fulfilling one or two of them."

She tipped her head, gave him a saucy smile. "Oh, I think you already have."

He kissed the lobe of her ear, nibbled at the soft part. "Which ones?"

"Um. I could tell you, but that could take a really long time." She smiled, took his hand, and tugged him toward the house. "Why don't I just show you?"

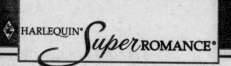

It's worth holding out for a hero....

*Three brothers with different mothers. Brought together
by their father's last act. The town of Heyday, Virginia,
will never be the same—neither will they.*

Tyler Balfour is The Stranger. It seems as if his mother
was the only woman in Heyday that Anderson McClintock
didn't marry—even when she'd been pregnant with Tyler.
So he's as surprised as anyone when he discovers that
Anderson has left him a third of everything he owned,
which was pretty much all of Heyday. Tyler could be
enjoying his legacy if not for the fact that more than
half of Heyday despises him because they think he's
responsible for ruining their town!

Look for **The Stranger**, the last book in a compelling new
trilogy from Harlequin Superromance and Rita® Award
finalist **Kathleen O'Brien**, in April 2005.

**"If you're looking for a fabulous read, reach for
a Kathleen O'Brien book. You can't go wrong."
—Catherine Anderson,
New York Times bestselling author**